DAKOTA BRAVE

Tales of the Territory

Lois Fichtner & Bill Kernan

Howard Jones

Published in association with
and distributed by:

P.O. Box 115
Superior, Wisconsin 54880

Spindrift Productions
Palm Harbor, Florida

Cover design
by Robyn Hillary

Library of Congress Catalog Card Number: 2001-126068
ISBN # 0-9702408-1-3
First Printing, 2001

© 2001 Howard W. Jones

Printed in the United States of America. All rights reserved. No part of this book may be reproduced in any form or by any electronic or mechanical means including information storage and retrieval systems without written permission from the author. Reviewers may quote brief passages in a review to be printed in a newspaper or magazine. For further information or to reach the author, please contact: Spindrift Productions, 305 Bay Street, Palm Harbor, Florida 34683

To order copies: Send $6.95 plus $2.00 for postage and handling to Spindrift Productions, 305 Bay Street, Palm Harbor, Florida 34683.

In the center of the continent, between the lakes and pine forests of Minnesota and the foothills terrain of Montana and Wyoming, lies the vast plain of the Dakotas.

Outsiders often think of the Dakotas as flat, bleak, dry, treeless and dreary. It's not like that, of course. There are hills, valleys, rivers, trees, lakes and the wonderful valiant people who live there.

At the time of these stories, our family had been on the land for three generations, plus we had a close link to earlier generations in the Dakotas via our friendship with the Sioux Indian children who attended our country school.

This book is about the people who discovered this land, and those who lived there during the depression and dust storms, enduring to raise new generations and bring the land to abundance. This book is dedicated to those brave people.

Some of the people in this book are still alive. If you find inaccuracies in these narratives, forgive me. I love you all, and mean no harm.

Author's notes:

This book is a mixture of fact and fiction: a fictionalized history.

The photo of the boys on the back cover was flipped so the fishing poles would be pointing "in" instead of off the page. Thus, the steering wheel is on the right — an unusual Model T Ford.

Also, the Indians on the front cover are Blackfoot, not Sioux. The Blackfoot also crossed this territory.

TALES OF THE TERRITORY

Celebration

The Immigrant

The Broken Dream

Injuns

Mister Brown

The Horses

The Well

The Hunters

Dust

Day of the Cows

Rocky Rogers

Beauty

Model T

Goose for Supper

Saturday Night

Spring

It's OK

Under the Pine Trees

— Celebration —

I was there for Groton's Anniversary parade.

The Governor and wife were in the first convertible, following the high school band. Next was a hay wagon full of "pioneers" with fresh-grown, long, gray beards. The wagon was pulled by one of the few teams of genuine work horses left in the area. Dawn Darlington, the town's unofficial hostess and cheerleader for fifty years, still regal, was in the second convertible with the Mayor. There were four more bands, and at least a dozen steam engines and lug-wheeled tractors.

My sisters were there, and dozens of my classmates. Several classes had impromptu floats. A rickety flatbed truck carried our class of '42. We were the noisiest. We shouted, laughed, and sang, jumping off to hug or shake hands with friends and old timers, and then back aboard again to shout and sing some more.

There was a giant barbecue picnic in the park, long lines for food (but enough for everybody), family groups, class pictures, a speech by the Governor,

"This town, this state has a great and proud heritage," he said.

"What do you know about all this history?" Pat Johnson asked me. "Your grand-dad was one of the first pioneers, wasn't he? And didn't your mother give talks about this area's history at the school?"

"Yeah, that's true."

"Well, write it down," she said.

"Maybe I will."

The Immigrant

Near Posen, in what was once West Prussia, then in succession the Polish Corridor, Nazi Germany, Communist East Germany, and now again Poland, was the tiny town of Gros Woelwitz. It was once a thriving farm village in a land of great Prussian estates, rich rolling farmlands and orchards. Now, I can't find it on the maps of Poland.

The Krueger family lived on a farm just outside the village. David and Anna Krueger, my great-grandparents, had five children, two daughters and three sons. The original family estate had shrunk as the generations progressed. Part of the loss was to division, as sons of earlier generations decided they couldn't live on the estate under the direction of a family patriarch, thus splitting it into smaller parcels. Some of it was sold to outsiders to satisfy the taxes levied by the parade of governments ruling the land.

There were efforts by family members to hold the estate together, to preserve the family tradition, as well as to maintain the efficiency of a major holding. But much of the land slipped away.

By the 1860's, there was not enough land to support the sons and prospective sons-in-law of David

Krueger. The family had to work out solutions for the problem.

Gottlieb, the youngest son, was gently pushed into the ministry. It was always good to have a churchman in the family. He took to it all right, married and raised a small, gentle family.

Paulina married a farmer's son from a neighboring village, and Hulda married a shopkeeper. They were provided with adequate dowries, painfully paid for with scrimping and sacrifice. That left three men at the farm — father David and sons August and Walter. One too many.

August, our grandfather, was the restless one. He was a reader, unusual for that family. He went to school as much as he could. There were long hours of work on the farm starting at the age of eight or nine, and limited school facilities. But he persisted. He had an interest in geography, in other countries and places. He dreamed about other lands — Argentina, America, Australia, the Orient.

One day when he was sixteen, he dared to launch the subject to his parents.

"Father, Mother, I want to travel, go to another country, to America. I will give up my share of the farm if you will give me some money so I can travel." The family was shocked but interested. It could be a solution to their problem.

August began to make inquiries, and went all the way to Zempelberg to get books and to talk to the stationmaster about a long journey. Gradually, a plan with a price developed. He told the family how much it would cost for the sea voyage, and for him to keep moving across America. He had read about the vast areas of rich farmland in America to be bought cheap or, amazing as it seemed, some of it even given away free to newcomers.

Herr Krueger, his father, thought about it for a week.

"I think you should go, August," he said one day. "It may not be what you think it will be. The free land may not be there. But you will see for yourself."

His mother cried a little and patted him on the shoulder. The family, the area and its generations had seen much travail and change. One had to be strong and brave — and enduring. Anna Krueger was all of those. She knew August should go. She doubted that she would ever see him again.

On a bright February day in 1868, after the previous year's harvest had been sold and the money had been raised for the tickets and a little more, August Krueger hoisted his canvas bag and his small trunk on a wagon train on its way to Posen and the railroad. The farewells were brief and tearful.

"Come back to us some day, August," his mother said, her eyes filled with tears. His brothers and sisters shook hands stoically. His father embraced him briefly.

"See America for me, August," he said.

The stationmaster at Posen, Herr Jeske, sold him the train ticket to Bremerhaven, where he assured August he would find a ship soon to sail for America. He gave the boy detailed information on how to find the ship, what class of passage he should pay for, about how much he should pay. Herr Jeske had been to Bremerhaven on a railroad pass, and had seen the ships. He had gone to the trouble of finding out how the people leaving his territory for foreign lands could make the connection. It was sad to see the young people leave. He knew most of them would never return. The least he could do, he felt, was to help them start their journey with the fewest mistakes possible.

He shook August's hand, gave him a kindly smile, and reminded him again how to make the ship connection. The train groaned forward and slowly chuffed out of the station.

He was amazed at Bremerhaven. He had never seen full-sized sailing ships, nor had he realized how big everything would be — the harbor, the ships and the sea beyond the harbor entrance.

He went to the office near the waterfront, described by Herr Jeske, and asked about a ship to America.

"We have a ship leaving in ten days for New York, Herr Krueger, if you have the money," he was told.

"I have the money for a low class ticket to New York, if it doesn't cost too much," August was always a good bargainer.

The ship's agent smiled at that. They haggled a bit, then struck an agreement. "You are going to America," the agent said.

August spent the ten days finding and reading books about America, and beginning to learn a few words of English language. By the day the ship sailed, he could pronounce with a thick Prussian accent, "hello," "good morning," "thank you," "please," "good bye," "help me," and a few other words.

Years later he told his family how the ship filled up with freight and German-speaking families — nervous young fathers and mothers with a brood of two or three little ones, a few older couples looking worried but determined, a number of single, young men like himself, their spirits swinging wildly from the great excitement of a new adventure to fear of the unknown, depression, sadness, and homesickness about leaving families and the land of their birth and youth — an aching longing already beginning to grow.

Grandfather always remembered that sea voyage.

He said the three-masted, wide-bellied freighter, with some holds converted to passenger space, hit the first swells of the North Sea with a sickening quarter-roll. She rolled like that for days while they fought the northwest breeze down toward the English Channel. By that time nearly everyone, including Grandfather, was deathly ill, rolling in the narrow, hard bunks, retching and running for the rail to heave dryly into the sea. The passenger quarters took on a sick, rotten smell that exacerbated the nausea.

Finally they were through the Channel, cleared the northwest coast of France, and started the long reach southwest toward the Azores. The wind was more behind them now. It began to get sunnier and warmer. The pale, haggard people started to come topside, one or two at a time. Grandfather walked the deck and sat against a hatch cover in the sunshine. He felt he had been delivered from a watery, foul-smelling hell.

As their strength returned, the voyagers began to wash and clean their quarters and their clothing. The ship came slowly alive. The steady wind drove the old, wallowing three-master along, night and day.

In two weeks they had passed west of Gibraltar, made the giant turn to the northwest, and picked up a steadily rising southeast trade wind, driving them toward North America. As they crawled north and west, the Atlantic again became irritable and abrasive, but most of the passengers had developed elementary sea legs, and began to lean into the rolls and pitches.

A week passed, and another week. Then one day the captain called the men passengers together. "We'll be in New York harbor in three days," he told them. "I want you passengers and your quarters to be spotless when they board us. Wash down your quarters every day, and wash all your clothing. I will assign a seaman to see that you have all the water and cleaning tools you will need. I will not have a dirty ship, or dirty passengers. It is for your own good to feel good and get through American Immigration. So, get busy and look your best for the Immigration Inspector," he smiled.

Grandfather said they were in pretty good shape by the time they passed through the Narrows and headed up the harbor to Manhattan.

Grandfather wanted to go west to St. Paul, Minnesota. His reading had informed him that St. Paul was the gateway to the new farmlands. He found he had enough money to get there, but very little more. He found a man who could speak German and got some information about the trip west. He slept on the floor of the train station with his bag under his head and his trunk against his back. His remaining money was in a leather pouch under his clothing, tied around his waist. He got through the pitiless, vicious city safely. The next morning he was on a train to Chicago, hungry, but riding a padded seat. He watched the countryside of lower New York State roll by for awhile, then fatigue took over and he slept until dark, and off and on for two more days.

He didn't stay in Chicago long. He was practicing his English and was able to make his way from one railroad station to the other. He found someone at the Union Station who could speak both German and English and learned how to keep going west. He eventually bought the cheapest ticket to St. Paul, Minnesota, and huddled down in a corner with his baggage to wait for the train. Before twenty-four hours had passed he was leaving Chicago and rolling west again.

St. Paul was still a frontier town in 1868 — it was a booming lumber town. The great pine forests covering the northern two-thirds of Minnesota and corresponding territory in Wisconsin were being harvested. The lumbering companies were aggressively recruiting the able-bodied immigrants who showed up in town. There were never enough lumberjacks to fill out the crews in the lonely lumber camps.

He resisted the temptation to sign on for high wages, compared to what he knew about wages in Germany. He wasn't a lumberjack; he was a farmer and he knew it. So, to earn money to continue his journey, instead of going lumbering, he took a job working for a grocery and hardware supplies wholesaler, unloading goods from the trains from Chicago and the stern-wheelers on the Mississippi, and hauling the goods to warehouses. Even on that job the wages were good. He lived frugally in a single room. In a couple of months he began to feel like a person of substance. He had a modest roll of American money. He could speak about a hundred American words, barely understandable through his thick, Germanic accent.

He didn't particularly like the work he was doing, but he was sturdy and willing. He was of medium height, but very strong. The lifting and loading was adding muscle to his stocky stature. His round face, with the high Slavic cheekbones, broad nose and wide mouth, was filling out, and he was experimenting with a mustache and beard, which were in fashion for young adults. He had thick, coarse, black hair, which he could barely control, but he kept it mostly out of the way with his roundish, foreign-looking cap. He began to add a few items of American clothing to his sparse Prussian wardrobe.

He worked for the merchant until spring, spending his evenings talking with other immigrants and with residents with whom he could converse, about the West, about farms and farmland. Also, he spent a lot of time looking for books, painfully reading everything he could find about the new frontier, again with a lot of help from new acquaintances. He had a friendly, diffident manner that brought sympathy and help most of the time.

One day in April, he made up his mind — he must move on westward. He very politely quit his job, left on good terms, and with a few hundred dollars in his pocket, he took a train west to the end of the line. At that time the rail line ended in West Central Minnesota. He spent less than a day in the tiny, pioneer town of Benson before a substantial-looking German with an accent even more pronounced than August's, approached him to ask about his plans.

The two talked easily in German, and in an hour or so, they had agreed on a kind of partnership. August would live and work with Earnest Radke and his family on their new homestead. Instead of regular pay, he would receive a share of the income from the farm. Earnest needed not only his new partner's farm labor, he also needed his intelligence and his superior handling of the language in the new world. Herr Radke may have suspected that August had more than a few American dollars in his pocket, dollars that would be very handy in expanding the farming operation.

The two shrewd, young Germans formed a friendly, businesslike, mutually cautious alliance. August invested the next two-and-a-half years farming with the Radkes, learning more and more about farming in America, and about how things were done in the new land. He bought his own farm of 80 acres nearby, but continued to live with the Radkes. Two more years went by. Nearly every evening he spent reading and studying to improve his English language capability and his store of knowledge of the new land.

When fall, then winter took over the prairie and the farm work lessened, he sought out the local schoolteacher, Augusta Erdmann, to help him read and study. He offered to pay her for her time but she refused. Instead, the two lonely, single people began to build a strong relationship. The Radke family, then the whole neighborhood started to remark on it.

When the school term ended in the spring of 1874, Augusta went home to Wisconsin. The next fall she was assigned to a different school nearly a hundred miles away. August practiced his new language skills by writing to her. She responded, so the relationship stayed alive. Nothing romantic, neither love nor marriage was mentioned, but it was implicit in the correspondence that Augusta and August might have a future together.

After the harvest of 1875, in October, a restless August decided to move west again. He was getting along fine with Radke. They had done quite well during the years they farmed together. But it was Radke's farm and Radke's family, not his own. August sold his 80 acres to his partner. He thanked Radke for having him and they parted friends. For years they would keep in touch by letter and eventually see each other again.

By this time August had acquired a light buggy and a good driving horse. He decided to travel northwest, alone, to Fargo. He had read and heard about the homesteading in North Dakota. He wanted to see what it was all about.

He stopped at lonely homesteads in Minnesota along the way, talking and visiting, bringing the news and getting news. He had become a gregarious man. He loved to talk and gossip, and laughed when he tried to match his thick German accent with an equally pronounced Norwegian, Swedish or Slavic brogue.

It got colder as he went north and west. Winter

was coming to the northern prairies. Already there had been a few snow flurries. He arrived in Fargo in early November, found a place for his horse, and a room in a boarding house for himself, then set out to see what was going on.

Fargo was a raw frontier town on the Red River of the North. At that time it was the end of the line for the Great Northern Railroad. The irregularly scheduled trains from St. Paul were bringing in whole households — women, children, cows, chickens, pigs, farm equipment and horses, all packed together in "immigrant cars." At the end of the line they were unloaded on the frozen prairie to find their way to the shanties and sod huts that would be their homes on the land claims until they could build something better.

August noticed that his former St. Paul employer, the wholesaler of groceries and hardware, had a sign and a small warehouse in Fargo. He went there and became acquainted with the manager, who told him they were going to continue to move westward ahead of the railroad, establishing distribution points in outposts that were being founded — Jamestown, Ellendale and Columbia. It was a friendly conversation. August felt he could work with this man.

He went to his room to think about it and the next day returned to propose that he contract to haul merchandise for the company to those western outposts. He had enough money to buy four good horses and a freight wagon. They talked it over and struck a deal. He was in business as a freighter on the frontier, an occupation that would satisfy his restlessness and wanderlust for a while.

Jamestown was ninety miles west, Ellendale more than a hundred southwest, and Columbia twenty-five miles south of Ellendale. That first late fall and winter he made two trips to Jamestown and one to Ellendale.

As the winter deepened, the northwest wind came sweeping down from the Arctic, across barren Canadian prairies, into the Dakotas with nothing to slow or deter its fury. Grandfather bought a great buffalo-robe coat, fur-lined mittens, heavy felt-lined boots and a fur cap. At times, out on the prairie, he was incredibly cold and lonely with only the brute animals for company. He would walk beside them to keep warm, gently talking to them as they slugged it out with the snowdrifts and the wind. Periodically, they would be caught in a blinding, choking blizzard. If he couldn't get to cover provided by the occasional cluster of winter-bare trees along a creek bed or an outcropping along a ridge, he would unharness the horses and huddle with them on the lee side of the wagon until the blizzard blew itself out. He survived, and eventually the brutal winter cold broke in favor of a raw and muddy, but warmer, prairie spring.

That summer he made his first freighting trip to Columbia in the James River Valley. He liked the country there. It wasn't as barren and flat as the land west of Fargo. There were willows along the James River and the creeks and small rivers draining into it. There was some protection from the prairie winds.

He hauled freight to Jamestown and Ellendale all spring and summer. In the fall of 1879 he made another trip to Columbia. At Columbia he turned his tired horses into a small, fenced pasture for a few days rest, and borrowed a riding horse from his friends there. He set out in a big circle, going southwest, then east, then north and back around to the west again. A half-dozen miles east of the James River he rode across some land he specially liked. It was flat, sloping gently toward the James River and to the valley of the Missouri, a hundred miles further west. The land there was empty, just a deep stand of prairie grass. There was no railroad in the area. The homesteaders and the developers hadn't arrived yet.

He thought constantly about that beautiful, gently sloping land as he and his team crawled back across the prairie to Fargo. He endured one more winter of hauling freight to Jamestown, Ellendale and the other new settlements beginning to come to life among the homesteaders, but he had made his decision. He was going to establish his empire on that piece of rich, flat prairie he had found.

In March he sold his horses and his freight business in Fargo for a good price. He withdrew his considerable bank balance and belted the bills around his middle once again. Then he bought a good horse and buggy and got ready to set out for Columbia where he had friends from his freight business, and where he could establish his temporary headquarters.

The day before he left he heard some news that changed his plans. When he went to say goodbye to his employer at the merchandise company, he was told that the Chicago, Milwaukee, St. Paul and Pacific Railroad, running westward about eighty miles south of Fargo, was going to extend its line on west another hundred miles to the James River Valley. August calculated that the rail line would run very near the rich prairie he had selected for his home.

He thought it over for an extra day. Then, instead of driving west-southwest to Columbia, he went straight south to the end of the Milwaukee Road rail line, now at Ortonville. In Ortonville, he again employed his natural, friendly curiosity and gift of gab. He talked with the railroad's surveying crew and with some of the construction managers. He learned that the plan was to establish a railroad station and town every six miles along the track heading straight west into the central part of Dakota Territory.

After digesting that information, he tied a rag around his left front buggy wheel and counted the turns of the wheel to where the next town site was marked. Satisfied that he could measure the distance between the intended stations, he started west. He was helped in checking his elementary survey technique at the beginning of the trip by the faint markers and stakes the first survey crew had set down. Some of the station sites were indicated. As he continued west, the survey work became less detailed, just a single line of stakes, far apart, showing where the rail line would go.

Six "towns" west he reached the top of a low range of hills, later to be known as the Antelope Moraines, and started down the long, gradual western slope toward the James River. At ten "towns" west, the land began to flatten out and take on the look of rich soil he was seeking. He kept going. After the twelfth station, he found no more town markings so he returned to the twelfth town, tied a rag to his buggy wheel and started to count.

At fourteen "towns" he stopped. He was, according to his reckoning, ninety-six miles west of Ortonville and about six or eight miles from the James River. The land was flat and rich-looking with no stones. He dug down with his shovel. The black soil went down more than a foot before giving way to a clay base. When the glaciers had withdrawn, much of this area was lake bed for a millenium or so. August didn't know much of the history or the geology of the area, but he knew soil and farming. He believed he was on the location of a future bonanza. He decided this would be his home, with the low hills to the east, and the flat prairie sloping ever gradually down to the river valleys to the west before rising again to the great peaks of the Rocky Mountains over the horizon. He marked the spot with a small excavation where his wagon wheel surveyor instrument told him the depot and town site would be, then looped out to search for a home site. A half-mile to the west, not far from the line of the railroad, he found the spot he liked. Then he stepped off the boundaries of what he thought would be his homestead claim.

He'd had plenty of time when he was farming in Western Minnesota and freighting in North Dakota to study the homestead laws. Each immigrant was allowed to make a claim on 160 acres. Then he or she must live on it for five years and raise some crops on it. That "proved" the homestead claim and the title to the land went to the homesteader. On the flat prairie of Dakota Territory, Congress added a codicil to the law. If the homesteader would plant ten acres of trees on another 160-acre plot of land, he or she could "prove up" ownership of this second quarter section.

For his "tree claim," he staked out the 160 acres directly west of his homestead claim. Then he prepared to drive his horse and buggy eighty miles southwest to Watertown, the nearest Federal land office.

Before leaving he made a decision on another matter. He had been continuing to write to his schoolteacher friend, Augusta Erdmann, who was still teaching school in Minnesota. He had told her of his plans for a home on the prairie, but prior to this, had not included her in his plans. She had answered his letters, so he knew she was still single and still interested in him. Now he decided to make a gamble on land, and on love.

Directly adjacent to his land, on the south side, he staked out another claim, to be entered with a "declaratory statement" of intention to file, to be held in the name of Augusta Erdmann. He then left to file his claims.

In Watertown, he successfully registered his own claims, and told the Federal official of his desire to enter a claim for Augusta Erdmann. The official told August the declaratory statement would hold the land for awhile, but that he should hurry to get Augusta to register. He would try to discourage anyone else from making a claim for the same parcel of land, and that perhaps August could also divert claimants away from the land in which he was interested in Augusta's behalf.

Then he found a room, brought his writing tablet from his luggage, and started a letter to Augusta. He had some news and a proposal for her. By evening the letter was finished. He went to the general store and post office, bought a stamp and sent the letter. Finally, he was ready for a good dinner and his first sleep under a roof for more than a week.

August had made a daring proposal to Augusta in his letter — that she come to Dakota, file her land claim and her tree claim, and if she liked the land and wanted to stay, they would be married. During the late summer and fall, as he divided his time between breaking up the soil for the next spring's planting and slowly constructing his new house, he was waiting impatiently for her response. He wanted to settle down, farm his land, and make a home. He was lonely. He wanted a mate.

No answer came that fall. He was persistent in his optimism. He wrote to her about the land, about the new town emerging around the depot, about the winter, and about going to a church meeting conducted by an itinerant Lutheran preacher.

That triggered it. Augusta wrote to him inquiring about the churches and school (there wasn't any), and what the people were like. August wrote another long letter telling her everything he could think of — about the people, the weather, how lonely he was. Again, daringly, he urged her to come out in the spring, in May when her schoolteaching was over for the summer to file her claim and see the territory. He told her the railroad by then would have reached within twenty-four miles of the town, named Groton by the railroad. He would meet her at the end of the rail line. He suggested she bring along a cousin, or her sister, for company and respectability.

One day in March, at the time of the first spring thaw, the mail buggy came from the rail head. The new storekeeper sorted the letters. In her letter to Grandfather, Augusta said she would come in June for a few days. He went about his work with a strange, warm glow inside himself.

That same spring there was another unusual episode in his new life on the prairie. Late one afternoon, a small caravan of tired people wound its way around the fledgling town from the east, and came to a stop on a meadow of unbroken prairie just south of the spot where Grandfather was building his homestead.

There were two adults, a man and a woman, three children and a small, pinto horse dragging a travois loaded with a bundle of skins and other packages wrapped in hides or pieces of blankets. The man was in the front, leading the horse. His main garment was a ragged gray blanket fastened in front at his throat with a long thorn or sharp stick. His hair was long, down to his shoulders, black and straight, parted in the middle and falling away from his face on both sides. On his feet were crude leather moccasins, coarsely sewn, without decoration. His whole appearance was somber and tired.

The woman wore a brighter blanket, red and gray, also fastened in front, but with a bright, beaded wooden needle. Her hair also was long, black and parted in the middle, falling away below her shoulders and tied between her shoulder blades with a leather thong. Both the adults had strong features, high cheekbones, and large, broad noses. Their eyes were black and intense, slightly almond-shaped.

The children appeared to range in age from seven or eight years to twelve. They wore leggings of various materials — skins or blanket cloth — blouses or shirts of the same materials, and short skin capes or blankets. August guessed there were two boys and a girl.

It was evening, nearly sunset when they stopped and began to set up camp. Grandfather watched them while he went about his work around his homestead, feeding his horses and the cow he had recently bought from another newcomer. Then the Indian man started across the field to where he was working. August advanced a few steps and watched him come. The man stopped a few paces from him, looked him steadily in the face and raised his hand, palm forward, in the gesture of greeting and peace.

Grandfather nodded, with a slight bow. He pointed to himself and said, "Krueger."

The Indian smiled and tried to repeat the word. "Kuger," he said.

Then Grandfather pointed at the man and said, "You?"

The tall Indian pointed to his chest. "Bear," he said. Then he made the unmistakable sign for hunger, rubbing his hand over his stomach with a circular motion. He pointed at Grandfather, then to his stomach, then to his family setting up the camp. Grandfather understood perfectly.

Grandfather looked at the man for a minute, thinking. Then he held out his hand to indicate the man should stay there, and went to his cabin. He wondered what he had that they would eat. He finally cut off a modest piece of cured ham he had bought, and filled a small cloth bag with coarse flour. He brought them out to the Indian, still motionless where he had left him. The man took the items, raised his arm in salute, and returned to his camp.

It was dark after he had eaten his own simple supper, but he could see a small fire where the Indians were camping. His natural curiosity drew him over to see the visitors. The children were out of sight; he could hear them talking and playing in the tipi shelter. The man and woman were sitting facing the fire. They both rose when he approached, smiling and nodding. He pointed to them, then pointed westward, to try to find out where they were going. A long, complicated conversation of signs and gestures ensued. The clearest information he could perceive was that they were traveling westward for four more days to visit others like themselves.

After a half-hour, he raised his hand in a farewell salute and returned to his shack. When he looked out the next morning at daybreak, they were packing up to leave. He watched them move off slowly and disappear in the distance on the great plain.

Over the years our family would be visited several times by this Indian family. Sometimes they were alone; sometimes other Indians were with them. Almost always the Bear family received food.

June finally came. Grandfather had broken more sod and planted nearly forty acres of wheat. It had been a hard, backbreaking spring working with machinery not quite big enough or strong enough. But he was learning how to battle the prairie.

He hitched a team of horses to a big, borrowed buggy and drove them to the end of the rail line the day before Augusta was to arrive; he wanted to be certain he was there to greet her. She did arrive the next day with her cousin, Emilie. Their greeting was polite and restrained. They hadn't seen each other for more than three years. They had never carried on like sweethearts, even when they were together in Minnesota. Grandfather was an enthusiastic, outgoing, emotional person. Grandmother remained essentially reserved all her life.

In this instance, they discussed the new country as they started west from the chaotic rail head in the big buggy. Augusta looked about her at the gently rolling, treeless prairie and thought about desolation. She was a little frightened and quite unsure about why she was there. Her decision to come to Dakota to meet this exuberant immigrant was made only after hours and hours of discussion with her family and other relatives and with her pastor, and then many more hours of agonizing indecision. She had her return ticket, and she hadn't made any promises, spoken, written or implied.

August talked excitedly about the new country for the next three hours while they jogged westward to the site of the homestead. He told of the quality of the land, the immensity of it, and about how much of it was available. Grandmother said when he talked about, it there was wonder in his voice. In Germany, they had been crowded on small plots that would barely make a garden in this new land.

They passed through the tiny, disorganized village that would eventually become the dominant trading town in the area. There were a few jerrybuilt frame buildings and several tents arranged along a space not yet well enough defined to be called a street, located roughly perpendicular to the survey lines for the new railroad.

"The name of this town will be Groton," August told them. "There is already a store. The storekeeper is Mr. Harnett. He brought his merchandise here by wagons. It is stored in a tent and in that building with a sign on it." They stopped at the shallow town well to water the horses, fill some water jugs, and to give the women a chance to look around.

Grandmother told us she had mixed feelings. Compared to the neat, established town in Wisconsin in which she grew up and still lived, this one was dirty and inadequate. On the other hand, to a twenty-three year old it was exciting, too. She literally tingled in anticipation of what was to come next.

The buggy rumbled and rattled over the rutted trail away from the raggedy little town, westward toward a low, ramshackle cluster of buildings a half-mile away. As they drew closer, they could begin to see the details of a tiny, rectangular building made of rough boards, a shingled roof, but no paint. Standing nearby was another low building shaped like a lean-to, with one high side and a sloping roof that descended nearly to the ground on the low side. Not a tree in sight.

"That's the homestead," August said, for the first time showing some apology and shyness. "I've got a lot of building to do. There is just enough to get by while I get some more land broken for planting next year. The square building is the house. The slanting building is a temporary barn."

The women couldn't help but look at each other with some wonder.

"Oh, you will sleep in the house. I will stay in the

barn while you are here." August seemed flustered.

"Do you have food?" Augusta asked. Her smile and little attempt at humor broke the tension.

"Yes, I have food. I will show you."

"Then we will cook," she declared. She smiled again, something that didn't happen often with her. She felt a small sense of relief. The whole situation had been strange and scary so far. Finally, she would be on familiar ground. Here was something she could do.

The visit began to improve. The tenseness started to dissipate as they climbed down from the buggy and walked around the tiny homestead. August opened the door and ushered them into the house. Just two rooms — a bedroom and a living-room/kitchen. It was clean, with cooking utensils and food containers neatly arranged on open, rough board shelves.

He carried in their satchels, then told them to make themselves comfortable while he took care of the horses and milked the cow. A half-hour later he brought in a pail of very fresh milk. The two women knew just what to do with the milk, dried foods, and dry, cured meat. As the summer dusk began to creep across the prairie, the incredibly delicious aroma of baking biscuits and frying meat drifted out from the cabin and filtered across the pungent barnyard. August smiled as he worked. The smoke from the tiny, wood-burning stove added its contribution to the rich, clean air.

"Come to eat," the call came from the cabin. He didn't recognize which voice it was, yet. He came in and sat down to a warm, exciting table. Augusta blessed the food and they ate. As it grew darker, August lighted the lantern, and the conversation became soft and close.

He told them about his plans, about the house he would build. He told them about the great reaches of land available and the deep, rich soil. He talked about the beginning of the town, who was there, and what he had heard about new people on the way. The women became interested, then fascinated, and the questions and answers flowed.

"The world needs grain," Grandfather told them. "Wheat, oats and barley to feed the people and the animals. This land will be giant fields of grain. We can make a fortune here." It was his first reference to an alliance between them.

The talk began to trail off as exhaustion overtook them.

"You must sleep," August told them. "Sleep as long as you like. I will sleep in the barn. I can get up early and work with the animals. Good night, ladies!" For the first time his gaze rested long on Augusta. She blushed and turned away.

With the lantern extinguished and the moonlight streaming in one of the two windows in the shack, the women whispered excitedly. There had been so much to see, so many surprises, the overwhelming idea of a marriage and living in this strange, empty land.

"Are you going to marry him?" Emilie whispered.

"I don't know. I just don't know. It is so big, so new, so much to understand. It frightens me; the whole thing frightens me. I almost want to cry."

"But marriage, Augusta! A man and a home, all this land, and children. It's an adventure. It could be wonderful!"

"I know. I know. But I'm still frightened."

The rising sun awakened them the next morning. It was going to be a gorgeous, fresh, early summer day. They could smell the rich aroma of the prairie. They heard August moving quietly among the horses, feeding, watering and currying them. When he heard movement in the shack, he began to milk the cow.

The girls lighted the stove, made quick, furtive trips to the outdoor toilet, and washed themselves in the semi-warm water heated on the reddening stove.

When he was sure they were dressed, August knocked on the door. Emilie opened it.

"Good morning, ladies. Fresh milk for breakfast."

Never had a breakfast seemed so delicious to August. It was only oatmeal with fresh milk and sugar, bread toasted on top of the wood stove and a cup of coffee. The difference was the two fresh, young faces, and the shy, embarrassed bustling about of the young women. It brought warmth and excitement to the plain board shack. He could hardly keep himself from blurting out his pleasure, and his love. This was his woman. He agonized over how she might feel about it.

"It is going to be a very nice day, I think," he told them, trying to use slow but perfect English diction. "I would like to spend the day showing you the land that is mine, and the land that could be yours. If you like the land, and if you want it, we will go to Watertown tomorrow and file your claim. Do you want to do it that way?"

The women were quiet for a moment, then glanced at each other.

"That will be all right, to look at the land," Augusta said after some hesitation.

August beamed at them and gently slapped the table top with his hand, a gesture he used all his life.

"That is fine," he said. "I will finish with the animals, then harness the horses. We will go in an hour."

He left the shack, going almost to the barn when he stopped, thought a minute, and returned to the cabin. He tapped on the door.

When it opened he had a shy smile. "Could we make a picnic to take along?"

Again the women glanced at each other and hesitated.

"We will fix a picnic," Augusta said.

It was a wonderful day. The prairie was in bloom. Wild roses, pink, white and red, pushed up from deep in the prairie grass. Daisies grew in clusters. The bright sunshine and a soft, sweet breeze produced an exhilarating environment.

"First we will see my land, then we will see what could be yours. We will see mine first so you can compare, and so you can see how your land would be next to mine."

He drove the team and wagon out of the yard, away from the homestead for nearly half a mile, to the center of a wide, slightly rolling landscape. August stopped the horses and pointed back toward the house.

"My land starts there, near the house, then goes over near that tree on the creek bed. Then it goes a half-mile over that way, then down a half-mile to where that little hill is. That is one quarter-section. That is my homestead claim."

The two women, used to wooded, rolling land with limited vistas, gasped.

"All that?" Augusta exclaimed.

"All that," August said with a smile. "That is only one claim. My other claim, my tree claim, is the same size. It is over there. We will drive the wagon to it."

It was more than a half-mile to the middle of the other claim, an equally rich, flat expanse of prairie.

"I will have to plant ten acres of trees on this land to make it mine. The rest of it I can farm. It is wonderful, rich land.

"Now I will take you to the land that I have asked to be saved for you."

Again it was a long wagon ride until he stopped a

half-mile directly south of his tiny homestead.

"This claim is a full quarter section directly south of mine…" His voice trailed away. "It is good land, Augusta. Just as good as mine. The railroad might cut across it, but that isn't so bad. It only takes out about two or three acres. It is worth that loss to have the claims next to each other."

He took a deep breath. "We could move the little house so it sets on the border between the two claims. Then you could live on your land and I could live on mine. Or we could have another claim shack on your land. We could spend half the nights on your land and half on mine. That way we could prove up both claims."

He stopped talking and waited. Augusta was looking across the green, grassy prairie toward the little, embryonic town. She didn't say anything. The silence became uncomfortable.

"There is one more thing," August said. "I have spent some time with the land people looking for a tree claim for you so you could have another quarter section of land. Two claims would be 320 acres for you, and I would have two claims making up another 320 acres. That is 640 acres for the two of us." He paused. "That would be a big estate in Germany, even in Wisconsin."

"Would you like to see your tree claim land? It is seven miles south of here, but we could be there in time for the picnic at noon."

Augusta was obviously struggling within herself. Her hand rose and fell again and again on the side of the wagon box.

"All right, we will go see it," she said finally.

August and Emilie both made gestures of relief, and the tension broke. August shook the reins to start the horses, and they headed across the prairie, follow-

August Krueger, Dakota pioneer.

ing a faint wagon track. The three young people began to talk and chatter and move about in the wagon. It was a long, rough, dusty ride, but it seemed short to Augusta.

Her mind was whirling. "Can I live in this giant, flat, treeless land? Do I love this man? Could I love him? Can I be married to him, live with him? It would be so far from home. Who would be with me if I had babies? Who would help me if I got sick? There's no doctor. I'm excited, but I'm frightened. What should I do? He wants an answer. I came all this way. Do I have to say yes?"

"Here we are, close to the right place," August's voice interrupted her reverie. "This isn't finally surveyed yet. but your tree claim would be just about here."

They got down from the wagon and walked stiffly about. August knelt and lifted a double handful of soil.

"This soil is lighter than on the main claim," he told her. "But it's good, rich land. It will raise good wheat and barley. It is valuable land." He sifted the soil through his hands, gazing into her face. In a moment she turned away and walked slowly across the prairie. As August watched her, his shoulders slumped.

"She doesn't want it," he said to Emilie.

"I don't know, August. She doesn't know. Don't push her so hard."

"But I want her. I need her here. This country won't be any good without her."

"Why don't you tell her that," Emilie said.

In a subdued mood, they ate their picnic lunch in the shade of the wagon, with the horses unhitched and tethered, grazing nearby. They rested awhile, then slowly walked about the land.

The long, rough ride back to the homestead was mostly in silence. When they arrived at the shack, they were tired and dusty. It was late afternoon.

"You ladies take all the time you want to wash up and rest. We can have supper late, or not have it at all."

"We will fix supper," Augusta said.

The sun was down when Emilie came out and told August that supper was ready. He washed at the well and came inside. Again there was a fine, simple supper, so warm and delicious compared to what he had been fixing for himself. After Augusta blessed the meal, they dug in with great gusto. Again there was a glow of comfort and fellowship in the rough cabin.

After supper, while the women were clearing away the dishes, and August was pretending to help tidy up the room, Augusta stopped her work and walked with determination up to our Grandfather.

"We will go and file the claims," she said.

August stared at her, dumbfounded.

Finally, he found his voice. "Augusta, are you sure?"

"Yes, I'm sure. We will file the claims. In the fall we will be married at my home."

"Oh, my God, Augusta. I'm so happy." He clasped her hands while Emilie pretended to be busy with the dishes.

So it began.

They were married and became a team. Workmates. He was the dreamer, the plunger, the talker, the politician. She was the steady, strong, quiet worker, the sober conservative balance wheel. There were five children and hired men to work in the fields, hired girls to help around the constantly expanding house. There was soon a new church in Groton. Her life revolved around family, home, work and church.

August became a major landowner of the new frontier. When other homesteaders, ill-suited for the sometimes brutal prairie weather and backbreaking work gave up, he would buy their claims — sometimes for as little as the price of the rail ticket back East.

In 1914, when he was sixty-four, August owned twenty-one quarter-sections of land in Dakota, thirteen in Montana and eight in Alberta, Canada.

Soon after he married, he changed from a pioneer farmer to a frontier entrepreneur. He roamed his land, visited the town with a fine horse and buggy, and supervised the work on his farms. The Kruegers had come full circle. There was again a major landowner in the family.

From this land, from Grandfather's estate, our Mother inherited our farm, eleven miles south of the original homestead.

The Broken Dream

Our Dad was a small, sinewy, energetic man. His left arm was withered at the shoulder but otherwise strong and muscular. He walked with a slight limp. Gradually, over the years Mother told us about Dad's youth in Minnesota and their life together. This is my reconstruction of her stories:

When our father, Frank, was a little boy on a farm in Southern Minnesota, the medics hadn't properly identified or named poliomyelitis, and Jonas Salk hadn't been born.

One summer when Dad was seven, he developed a sudden soreness and stiffness in his back and arm. There was great pain and finally a loss of strength in his left side, eventually concentrating into an almost total paralysis of his left arm and leg. His parents attributed the illness to his having fallen asleep one afternoon outdoors on the damp ground, and thus had contracted a violent rheumatism.

Little Frank became very, very ill and feverish, day after day, then week after week. His left side was motionless, his left arm paralyzed. He didn't get better, as expected. Instead, he got slowly, inexorably worse until the country doctor told his parents that hope for his survival was nearly gone.

Staying with the family was John's sister, Blodwyn, young Frank's aunt, who helped nurse the weak, sick little boy. She became increasingly involved in his illness and pain. She questioned God's plan. Why make this little boy suffer so? She set about trying various kinds of care. She was not a nurse; she simply applied her frontier common sense, plus what she had read and heard about various medical cures.

The boy seemed more comfortable when she applied hot compresses to his stiff left leg and paralyzed arm. She gradually increased the application of wet heat because it seemed to soothe him, reduce the pain and sickness, and allow him to rest. Also, for some reason the application of heat seemed to gradually bring down his fever. She extended the application of heat to his entire body. She thought she saw a slight improvement in his condition, a tiny positive response. He had been ill for nearly two months. She asked his mother if she noticed a change.

Mary, young Frank's mother, was an intelligent, loving, uneducated woman. She had two smaller children, a husband working desperately to farm the land and build a life for his family, and a primitive, pioneer farmhouse to look after. She spent as much time with Frank as she could, but was relieved to delegate primary responsibility for his care to her sister-in-law. She was terribly distressed about the little boy's mysterious illness, but she had to allocate her time and energy to her heavy responsibilities. She told Blodwyn she thought the treatments were helping, and asked her to continue to care for him. At night she prayed tearfully to her God to forgive her if she wasn't doing enough. She hoped He realized she was doing as much as she could.

Blodwyn received the encouragement to continue

her treatments as an endorsement of her efforts. She treated it as an affirmation of her responsibility to try to cure the boy with all the strength of her sturdy character.

Blodwyn and the doctor discussed ideas for treatment. Dr. Adams was incredibly busy, traversing the countryside with his horse and buggy, handling the critical cases as best he could — numerous broken bones, great cuts and bruises, all the traumatic injuries of a frontier farming community, childbirths by the dozen, diagnosing and treating illnesses and performing crude surgery as best he knew how. The mysterious illness of little Frank Jones was not new to him. He had seen it run its inevitable course several times and take the lives or hopelessly cripple its small victims. Neither he nor the other doctors with whom he talked or corresponded about it had a successful treatment. He had sadly written off this case as one more tragic mystery still to be enlightened by medical research and discovery. He gave Blodwyn the best advice he had for making the boy as comfortable as possible.

Blodwyn began massaging Frank's left arm and leg, as a loving gesture, but also to see if he might possibly respond. Every day she would work with his limbs for an hour in the morning and an hour in the afternoon. Sometimes he was restless, sometimes he cried, sometimes he fought her, but she persisted. The will and strength she drew upon to keep this up week after week, with no assurance it would bring any improvement, was a wonder to her sister-in-law and her brother. They thanked her again and again for her willingness to keep trying, and praised her for her care and concern.

She talked to Frank about it. "It's going to be hard. It may hurt awful. You must have courage. You have to fight. You can't give up."

The boy did respond. It was autumn now. Although his left arm was still completely paralyzed, he was now moving his left leg, bending it slowly at the knee, then slowly, with agony, straightening it out. He could move the foot from side to side. The leg was emaciated, weak and painful, but Blodwyn's strength and persistence were slowly being transmitted to the boy. Now he, too, was determined to be healthy again, to walk.

His appetite improved. His eyes became brighter and he sat up often, with help. In October they lifted him into a chair. He was able to sit weakly upright. In November she tried to get him to stand with some weight on his left leg. He tried it, but cringed and cried with the pain. His leg wouldn't hold him, so she continued massaging.

They made a pact that he would try to take his first steps on Christmas morning, a present for his parents. It was a specific, inspiring goal. He tried harder. He took three steps with his left leg that Christmas morning. He cried out in pain, and he cried when it was over. Both his mother and his Aunt Blodwyn hugged and praised him.

His father put his big, rough hands on each of Frank's arms.

"You have come back to us, son. You have come back from the dead. God has helped you and your Aunt Blodwyn to save yourself. We are very happy and proud of you."

His progress picked up momentum from that day. During his years at the country grammar school, he was usually carried to school by his father or pulled in a cart by his brothers. He limped terribly. His left leg dragged when he walked. His left arm was limp and helpless. He continued the program started by his Aunt Blodwyn, who was now married and living several miles away. She would try to visit the Jones family once a month to encourage Frank to keep on with his exercises.

When he was in high school, he began to walk almost normally, with only a slight limp. He could move the fingers of his left hand, but could barely lift the arm as high as his waist.

For farm boys such as the Joneses, a half-dozen years of education was often the extent of it. Their future was almost always to become farmers. Two of Frank's brothers didn't finish high school; they became bored with education and took jobs with other farmers, something which could eventually lead to marriage and a farm of their own.

Frank's situation was different. It appeared to his parents that he would never be able to perform the exhausting, heavy labor that was a primary ingredient of farming. What could he do?

It was traditional for every family to produce a minister. They discussed that idea with Frank. He wasn't interested.

"I want to be a teacher," he told them. "I like mathematics and science, and I'd like to teach those subjects."

The parents thought it over and reluctantly agreed. Instead of a farm, Frank would get a college education. He was the first person in that family to have one. He emerged from little Valparaiso College with a teaching degree and a left arm that could hold and lift. It was a little shorter than the other arm and it was weak, but it was working, and getting stronger every year. He was a top student.

Frank Jones got a job teaching in a small high

school, then a year later in a larger school. Several successful years passed. He loved teaching. He was exceptionally good at it. Based on his reputation for solid teaching and firm discipline, he was hired by the Red Wing "reform school" for unruly boys to be a teacher and monitor. He taught there for two years, gaining the respect of both his students and his superiors.

Along the way he heard about the exciting frontier-like Dakotas, now establishing significant towns and schools. He decided he would like the challenge of the new land, so he traveled there one summer and got a job in a new, small high school in Ipswich, South Dakota. It went well, and the second year they asked him to be Principal.

The School Board also hired a new language teacher for the same school year that Frank Jones became Principal. Her name was Lydia Krueger. Frank was thirty-one, Lydia was twenty-one. An attraction between the two developed steadily throughout the year. Because it was a very small school in a tiny town, they could show very little interest in each other. Glances and a few fond words were all they dared. Even so, there were a few snickers and some gossip — there wasn't much else to talk about in such a small town.

The next summer there was a four-day teacher's convention for Eastern South Dakota. With the greatest propriety, and with a hundred other teachers looking on, their courtship began in earnest. There was never any doubt about how it would come out. They were meant for each other, they both knew it.

One teacher, a special college friend of Lydia, commented on Frank's arm.

"Is there something wrong with his left arm, Lydia? It seems shorter or different than the other one."

"It is shorter. He had a sickness when he was a

little boy and it was paralyzed for awhile, but it is all right now."

"You should know, Lydia," she giggled.

In August of 1914 two events happened that profoundly affected the lives of Lydia and Frank. August Krueger died of cancer rather suddenly at a time when his land empire was growing and prospering at its zenith. His will gave each of his children three quarter-sections of land. Augusta, his wife, received four quarter-sections, plus all his land in Montana and Alberta.

After the funeral Augusta, talked to Lydia. "You have land now. It is valuable. You should live on it, farm it, and raise a family. You should be married."

"But he hasn't asked me yet, Mama. He loves me, I think, and we have talked about marriage, but nothing specific yet."

"Well, write to him. Tell him about Papa, tell him about the land. Tell him you need a husband."

"My goodness, Mama, I can't do that. It isn't proper."

"Proper, proper. This no time for proper. Write to him, Lydia"

Lydia was saved from her embarrassment because the next day Frank Jones was there. He had been restless at his home in Minnesota, longing to see and talk with the woman he loved. He decided to come back to his school several weeks early, ostensibly to get ready for the new school year, but actually to come by the Krueger home to visit Lydia.

He was saddened to hear about the death of her father. Frank and August had enjoyed some very good talks. August loved to talk, to listen and learn, and Frank Jones was an intelligent, educated person. Lydia told Frank about the will.

"Mama thinks I should take over my farm."

"You, Lydia? You can't do it. You have to have a husband. That's me. Will you do it, Lydia? Will you marry me?"

Lydia buried her face in her hands, laughing and crying. "Of course, Frank."

They were married on the Krueger farm three days later. Lydia's brothers stopped their work in the harvest fields long enough to stand sweatily while the ceremony was performed.

Their move to the farm was delayed for several years, first while they finished their school term contracts and then when they were side-tracked to Montana for nearly three years of teaching, homesteading and working in a bank in the frontier town of Winnett. The South Dakota farm was rented to a relative during the Montana adventure.

The farm they inherited, and finally inhabited, was three contiguous quarter-sections with a homesteader house and some small barns.

It was a tiny five-room house — kitchen, dining room, living room, small bedroom and tiny half-bedroom. Gradually, over the years, the house grew to accommodate our growing family. First came an enclosed porch for the engine-driven washing machine, the cream separator, space for canning and butchering, and a place to wash off the mud and dirt from the fields and barnyards before entering the house proper. Later came another addition on the other side — a sleeping porch for visitors and sometimes a sewing room. It was reasonably warm in the cold winters, with the kerosene space heater close by the door. As more children came, and began to grow up, dormer windows were put into the upstairs, and the attic became a sleeping room for the girls.

It was home, a haven, protection from the some-

*Frank and Lydia Jones
at the time of their marriage.*

times-raging weather of the raw prairie. All seven of us lived there, squeezed together in a space that today wouldn't be considered fit for more than three or four people.

Home it was. Home from school after the long two-and-a-half mile walk across the land. Home from the bone-chilling, all-night field work in the spring. Home from sub-zero, paralyzing work with the animals in the winter. Home from the hot, dust-choked exhaustion of harvesting in late summer.

A wood stove in the kitchen, a kerosene heater in the living room, no heat in the bedrooms. We children would dance across the icy floor from the warm blanket beds to huddle close to the heater while getting dressed in winter. In summer my sisters could lean out of the window of the one upstairs room at dawn and smell the ripening wheat surrounding the house.

That house leaked rain, if it ever rained. It leaked air and dust, even a little snow. It was built without insulation. We didn't know about modern insulation until years after we lived there. When the sub-zero, northwest winds howled across the prairie in winter, that little house creaked and strained and stopped the wind as best it could. It let a lot through, of course. The family dusted the snow off their blankets and turned the kerosene heater up another notch, until we ran out of kerosene. Then we would stuff more wood into the kitchen stove until the stovepipe glowed red.

We didn't get a radio until the dust bowl years were over. Our parents thought good books and recordings of classical music were higher priorities than a radio. My sisters and I mourned our isolation, begging for a break in the monotony of life on the remote farm.

On cold winter nights, lonely neighbors would gather in our kitchen. There was Mick, a young man from Germany and a relative of my Mother, with his two-week beard, thick guttural accent and chuckling good humor. Mister Brown was our part-Indian hobo farmhand. There was Rocky Rogers from a mile south, and the Jensen boys. They would hunker down against the kitchen wall, politely declining the chairs my Dad would offer, and talk about farming, the weather and politics. They would spin yarns of pure fabrication, laugh at each other's lies, and sometimes talk about the old days.

Rocky Rogers and John Jensen, the oldest of the group, could remember when there were still bands of Sioux Indians moving across their land from the lake country in the low hills to the east, toward the Missouri River and the reservations a couple hundred miles to the southwest. They yarned about the few years of the great bonanza wheat crops, when it appeared that everyone would become rich, and about how it all came crashing down along with the stock market, and now was blowing away with the drought and dust.

We children would roost on the benches and chairs on the other side of the archway into the tiny dining room, inhaling the rich aroma of barnyard from the men's boots, smoke from the roll-your- own cigarettes and left-over smells from the supper just finished, raptly listening to the conversation stimulated by the fellowship of the warm kitchen.

The talk would rumble on, each man hating to return across the cold prairie to his lonely shack. Then finally, Mother would motion us children off to bed, and the visitors would reluctantly stub out their cigarettes, pull on overshoes and mittens, and say goodnight.

There were five of us children. Ruth was born in 1917 and Frances in 1919 in Montana. Mary came in 1921 and I was born in 1924. Helen, the "afterthought," was born in 1930. Mother had a doctor in attendance when the two girls were born in Montana. When Mary, the third child was born, mother went to stay with Grandma Krueger in Groton. Dr. Hart came to Grandma's house for that one. She never went to a hospital. It was too far away, nearly a half-day drive on muddy roads. Most of the childbirth care was in the hands of Grandma Augusta and Mrs. Milne, the midwife.

When it was time for my birth, it was a busy season — corn harvest. Mother decided to stay home and trust that Dr. Hart would get there in time, over rough gravel and dirt roads via his trusty Model T Ford. For a back-up, a nervous cousin, Esther Erdmann, looked after the little girls and stood by to deliver the baby if Dr. Hart didn't make it in time.

I was told the baby (me) arrived several minutes ahead of the doctor. He breezed in full of good cheer and jokes, did his snipping and cleaning, watched the mother and baby for an hour and breezed back to town. The next morning Dad carried me outside to show me to the corn harvesting crew.

Dr. Hart got there in time for my sister Helen's birth. His Model A Ford was that much faster than the old Model T, and the roads were improving. He had time for a cup of coffee and a crude ham sandwich fixed by my Dad after midnight before he had to help bring the new life into the world.

In the 1920's life went well on the farm. The work was very hard, probably excruciatingly hard at times for our father with his weakened side. He never mentioned it, never complained. He never in any way ever implied that he might be happier in classrooms teaching math and science.

Once in awhile, on Sunday night or a holiday,

Dad would bring out his math books and spend an evening working problems at the dining room table. When Mother noticed, she would stop her busy work with us children and the house, come over to him and put her arm around his shoulders. He would look up at her, pat her arm, and the moment was over.

We went to school in a tiny, one-room country schoolhouse. The teachers, usually 20 or 21 years old, sometimes younger, did the best they could after one year of training at the "Teachers College." Actually, we learned more at home than at school. Our parents, both ex-teachers, gave us as much time and teaching as their busy lives would allow. It was a strenuous, happy life.

In 1929 we read and heard all about the stock market "crash." It didn't affect the life on a South Dakota farm very much right away. But then the Great Depression came on in the eastern states. Farm prices began to fall and interest rates on the loans farmers depended on for seed, other supplies and machinery remained high.

Still, our family, with our financial welfare based on our ownership of the land, continued to get along reasonably well. But, in 1931, it didn't rain. There was virtually no grain crop to sell, and meager feed for the animals.

The drought extended through 1932. Nothing much grew and the land started to blow. Great clouds of dust rolled across the landscape, blotting out the sun. Some farms were already failing, the families giving up and moving away. Our Dad and Mother squared their shoulders and, tight-lipped, fought the land and the weather. They intended to survive on the land, no matter how brutal the game.

Our Dad didn't smile very much in 1932. There

were deep vertical lines in his face, tracing from beneath his deep-set eyes down past his mouth, nearly to his chin, like long, deep dimples. "Smile lines," we called them. He had smiled when he was younger, and before the drought and depression had overwhelmed him on the plains. He had been happy, well-adjusted in his teaching. He loved teaching. He loved his wife and children. He tried to smile for them. It was a strained, forced smile, almost painful to see. The disaster on the prairie had hit him hard.

He had dreamed and envisioned a prosperous farm, a comfortable, busy estate, a home for his growing family. He had seen a productive, growing plantation on the prairie that would form a permanency, a foundation and a legacy for his family. He had decided in 1927 to make a strong gamble, and had mortgaged the land for money to build modern barns for the animals, shelters for the machinery, and sturdy fences around the big pastures. Prices were outrageously high for labor and materials in 1927, '28 and '29, but Frank and Lydia decided to pay the price to build their dream.

But as the economic crash rattled and thundered across the land, prices for beef, eggs, cream, wheat and barley tumbled to almost nothing. The bank loan, for which our Dad had pledged the land, seemed gigantic, monumental, compared to the puny prices received for the farm's production. The value of the land itself withered away as the drought and depression deepened, until the value of the whole farm was less than the loans owed for putting up the buildings and fences.

The bankers, desperate to keep from going under, began calling in their loans, loans that were made to reliable people such as Frank and Lydia Jones, who now couldn't possibly pay them back. There just wasn't any money. Savings accounts, revenue from animals and crops, money from relatives in less desperate economic circumstances, all went to try to pay down the loans, but none of it was enough.

The banks started foreclosing on the nearly valueless land, grabbing anything they could to add to their disappearing assets. They then sold the land to one of the few institutions in the country that still had money — insurance companies. Those bargain hunters accumulated millions of acres of once-valuable farmland, holding it against the day when the cycle would turn upward again.

Many of the banks went under, taking the savings and deposits of their customers with them. The Brown County Bank in Groton closed (it was later bought and re-opened by a larger bank). Our parents didn't have many dollars in the bank to lose. We heard from them that Grandma Krueger lost all her savings, but with her ownership of the land in Dakota, Montana and Alberta, she recovered well enough to maintain her modest lifestyle.

Under the economic programs of the Roosevelt administration, many of the banks reorganized and re-opened. The insurance companies, with deep enough cash foundations to weather the storm, survived. In the l940's they made killings selling the land they had acquired so cheaply in the depths of the depression back to the farmers.

Our farm became the property of Mutual of Omaha, a small, conservative company. They knew the eventual value of farmland. It didn't go so badly for our family. The insurance company took one-third of the crops for rent. In return, it made minor improvements on the farm. Buildings were repaired when necessary, and painted at long intervals.

After the supervisors from Mutual of Omaha got

to know our Dad and learned that he could no more cheat them than he could his own family, they stayed away almost entirely. Just an annual goodwill visit to renew the leases, look at the buildings, and visit with Dad and Mother about next year's farming plan. In our case it was a fair, friendly relationship, not the raw, adversarial, threats and thunderous situations some of the neighboring farmers had with their new landlords. Most of these families were second-generation pioneers, whose parents had settled and proved up their land. Having "outsiders" supervise their life on the land was bitter medicine.

When the land was lost, it was a terrible time for our parents. Dad had taken full responsibility for Mother's inheritance of the early 1920's. Together they had planned its expansion and improvement, but Dad had felt a personal obligation for its preservation. We learned all this from our Mother as we grew old enough to understand.

When the inheritance started slipping away, and then when he knew they were going to lose it, Dad almost went crazy with desperation and despair. Mother later told us there were times when Dad didn't seem to sleep for days at a time. He would get out of bed, dress, and roam the land in the dark, trying to think of ways to save it. He worked like a madman, doing the labor of two or three men, trying with his muscles and sinew to overcome the disaster.

But everything failed. There was no way, human or inhuman, that he alone could overcome the dust-choking, stomach-wrenching physical and economic desolation. His health deteriorated. Even when healthy, he was a small, wiry man with a withered arm. What there was of him was all sinew and determination. We children all admired his strength and energy. But his

*Our parents, Frank and Lydia Jones,
on the farm in 1940.*

system ran down, and physical breakdown attacked him.

He developed a giant infection on the back of his neck that became a gaping, open wound. The ill-equipped country doctor couldn't do much with it — this was before the time of penicillin or antibiotics. All the doctor could do was to clean it, apply an antiseptic and recommend rest. Dad couldn't rest. He was losing the family's farm and soon they would want for the basic necessities of life.

Finally, he became too weak for the heavy labor of the farm, and then lapsed into a semi-delirious state. At least he was finally in bed, resting. Mother wasn't sure he could pull through. His strength, his color and his will to live seemed to be gone. She nursed him, coaxed him to eat nourishing broth, then solid food. Most of all she encouraged him. She told him again and again that it didn't matter. They had each other and the family, and that was everything.

In the great tradition of the frontier and the prairie, the neighbors provided the labor to keep the farm going, feeding the animals, milking the cows, bringing supplies that were sometimes paid for with their own desperately meager means. Mother's cousins, the Erdmann family, provided most of the help to keep the Jones family going.

Slowly, slowly, through a long winter, Dad started to heal. He could sit up, then get out of bed and move about the house, then go outside to do light chores. He had survived. With his survival came a cleansing of his fevered, desperate frame of mind. After being so near death, the loss of the farm became less monstrous. He could accept it. Mother, whose land it had been, had never considered the land as important as the welfare of her husband and children. She would have given up the farm with no hesitation if Dad had indicated an inclination to go back to teaching.

By spring, our Dad was back operating his struggling spread. His determination was back. Somehow they would beat the depression and the drought. They would still be there when the drought was over, when the national economy came back, and when prices for the farm's production were again high enough to allow them to farm at a profit. It was the beginning of the painful trip back. There would be more setbacks, more despair, but we would live through those seemingly impossible problems.

Dad even had another health crisis. While his system was still weak from the year-long battle with the giant infection, he got another one. This time a barley beard got stuck in his eyeball and began to fester. Facing a new episode, Mother insisted that he go right to the small regional hospital to save his life for his family. Again came massive infection, weakness and delirium. But this time, with rest and care, he was back at his work in three months. Again our wonderful relatives and neighbors helped us through the crisis.

Mother was so different from our Dad. Dad was a nervous, small man, driven to accomplish and excel — a typical Welshman. Mother's German forebears gave her a strong body, practical intelligence and the determination to carry on and on. Looking back on it, when they were retired and living in relative ease, she told us she couldn't believe she had endured and survived the trials and abuses of the 1930's on that dry, lonely farm.

She had loved being a teacher. She hated the loneliness, the dust and dirt, the privations and poor facilities available for her family on the farm. As would any good farmer, Dad built up the productive parts of the operation first: barns for keeping and milking the cows and housing the horses and pigs, and buildings to protect the machinery. Last came a new house for the family.

The basement was dug, the foundations poured, and part of the building materials stockpiled before the economic crash and the dust storms hit us simultaneously.

Those beginnings of the new home lay there under our eyes throughout the years, mute testimony to the broken dream.

Injuns

I stood on the porch of the tiny, one-room schoolhouse, gazing toward the southwest, past the Benson's place, past another half-mile of rolling pasture, to where a horse with two riders had just come slowly over the horizon. The horse walked steadily toward me, following the low country road, growing larger. In five minutes I could see that the horse was a brown and white pinto. In another five minutes I was sure the riders were a boy and girl, riding bareback. Freddie Sanders had just arrived from the other direction and sidled up beside me.

"The new kids are comin', Freddie. I wonder what they'll be like."

"I heard they was Injuns. Just moved on to the old Strong place. What the hell we gonna do with a couple 'a Injuns?" Freddie asked softly.

We scuffed restlessly back and forth, stepped off into the small schoolyard and threw stones across the road into Benson's pasture. It was March. The winter was beginning to fade, revealing patches of brown grass and earth. The low road was almost clear of snow. The pinto with the two children aboard had reached the Benson's driveway, coming straight for the school, still at a steady, brisk walk.

Freddie went to the schoolhouse door, stuck his head inside and gestured. Phyllis and Doraine Benson came out to stand beside us on the porch.

"Lookit here what's comin'," Freddie said. "New kids. Injuns. Watta ya think about that?"

"You don't know they are Injuns, smarty," Doraine said. They stood quietly watching the horse and riders approach. When they were just a quarter-mile away, Phyllis went inside with the news.

"The new kids are comin', Miss Bjerke. Looks like they're Injuns all right."

Miss Bjerke came out to the now-crowded little porch, together with the other four pupils. "All right, children, let's not stand here and stare. Let's go inside and get ready for school."

I asked, "Can me and Freddie stay out here an' make sure they know how to put the horse away?"

A tiny smile flickered at the corners of her mouth. "All right, you two stay out and help them."

We stayed on the porch and stared as the horse, ears alert and forward, turned into the schoolyard. I noticed that the horse had a light, well-worn bridle with scuffed reins that looked as if it may have had long, hard use and perhaps had lain out in the weather most of the time.

The pinto was lean and a little small, but appeared to be strong and lively. The boy on the horse pulled him to a stop, motioned to his sister, and she slid down, gripping her syrup-can lunch pail by its wire handle, never looking at us on the porch. She had on a wrinkled winter jacket over a straight print dress. Gray stockings went down to old-fashioned, brown shoes that appeared to be too big for her

Her hair, thrusting down from under a gray stocking cap, was jet black and straight, cut off square just below her ears. Her face was round and very dark. She wasn't pretty, except for her eyes — round, dark and glittering.

While we stood on the porch and stared silently, she stood motionless, eyes to the ground. Her brother walked the horse to the shed-style barn near the back of the school, jumped down lightly, and led the horse inside. In a minute he was out, carrying his own lunch pail. As he walked past his sister toward the porch, he gestured roughly for her to follow, and stepped up on the porch. The boy also wore a winter jacket over bib overalls, and a red and gray flannel shirt. The overalls were too wide for him and too long, turned up at the bottoms of the legs. I thought he looked to be about eleven years old, with a good-looking, sharp-featured face with high cheekbones and flashing black eyes. Even in the too-big clothes he seemed to be tall and strong.

He looked squarely at us, but nobody spoke, and they brushed past and entered the school. Freddie and I looked at each other. Freddie made an exaggerated shrug and we, too, went inside.

Miss Bjerke rose from behind her desk when the two new children entered the schoolroom. She was a smallish, compact person in her early twenties. I thought she was beautiful. Her short, curly hair, fair skin with light make-up, plaid skirts and wooly sweaters made her a princess compared to the weather-beaten, hard-working women and girls on the farms and ranches.

"Hello, children," she greeted the newcomers. "Welcome to Garden Prairie School. I'm Miss Bjerke." The Indian children stood mute. "You may hang your jackets there by the door. We have a good desk for each of you." Her tone was kindly and gentle.

The boy deliberately took off his jacket, hanging

it where the teacher had indicated, and gestured for his sister to do the same. Then he turned to face the teacher and the school. His sister stood behind him, eyes on the floor.

"Would you please tell us your names, and which grades you are in?" Miss Bjerke asked.

"My name is Johnny Bear Day," he said flatly, and paused. The children grinned when he gave his name, and somebody snickered. He stood rigid with tension, and stared them down. "Her name is Geneva," he continued. "We haven't been goin' to school regular. She's in about the second grade and I'm in the fourth or fifth."

Miss Bjerke hesitated a moment, absorbing the information. "Well, we can talk later about what grades you should be in. Now, I want you to meet the other children."

She moved to the rows of desks and touched each child on the shoulder as she introduced them. "This is Edith Sanders, Phyllis Benson, Mary Jones, Howard Jones, Freddie Sanders, Betty Benson, Doraine Benson and Leon Krueger." Johnny Bear stared at each child as their names were given. His sister didn't look up from the floor.

"Now please take your seats, Geneva here in the first row by Leon, and Johnny over there between Howard and Phyllis," she directed, pointing to the empty desks.

The school began to settle into its morning schedule. Miss Bjerke spoke softly with Johnny and Geneva, trying to determine exactly how far they had progressed in school. We all listened carefully for snatches of the conversations. Eventually she gave them books and notebooks, telling them the supplies were temporary until she could request their proper textbooks from the office of the County Superintendent of Schools. Johnny Bear drew pencils and a pad of paper from his overalls, gave one pencil and a few sheets of paper to Geneva, and they were ready to start learning.

One great advantage of the one-room country school was that each child could, if he or she was curious and so inclined, listen to virtually all the classes taught in the school. Students who might get tired of the lessons or exercises to which he or she was assigned, could stop and listen to fourth grade arithmetic or sixth grade geography for awhile. Thus, the learning was reinforced many times over the eight years of country school.

At lunch time we gathered with our lunch pails on the sparse, new grass against the side of the schoolhouse, glad to be outdoors, even in the cool weather. Johnny and Geneva sat aside from the other children, who were watching intently. The Indian children left their lunches in their pails, and quickly stole bites of pieces they drew out, — rough sandwiches filled with thick, ragged pieces of meat. They ate silently, while the others began to chatter and laugh, as they normally did at lunch time.

Finally, the lunches eaten, I walked over and stood in front of Johnny. "That's a pretty nice horse you were ridin'. Looks like he could run pretty good if you let him. Where'd you get him?"

The Indian boy sat staring up at me, saying nothing. Finally, he put the cover on his lunch bucket and stood up, facing me. He was slightly taller and bigger than me. He was again rigid and tense.

"Didn't steal him," he said flatly.

"Jeeze, I didn't mean nothin' like that," I said. "I just thought he was a good horse."

Johnny Bear stood staring at me. I thought he was

going to hit me. Then he relaxed, bent down and picked up a stone, and threw it far out into the prairie grass. "He is," he said.

We all began to move around, seeking an outlet for the morning's pent-up energy.

I decided to try again. "We're all goin' to play some kitten ball. You wanna play?"

Another long pause, while Johnny Bear looked from one of us to the other. "I'll try," he said finally. "She won't." He gestured toward his sister who still sat with her back to the schoolhouse, looking at the ground.

Johnny Bear didn't talk much during the game. He could catch the ball, though, and was a very fast runner. When it was his turn to bat, he hit a long fly-ball far beyond the farthest fielder.

"You musta played this game before," Freddie said.

"Naw, but we played some games somethin' like it. Indian games," Johnny answered.

As the days and weeks of early spring progressed, Johnny Bear, Freddie and I started doing things together, playing ball, trapping gophers, teasing the girls, digging caves, and building forts in the dirt bank along the road in front of the school. We became good friends. We waited impatiently for the recess periods and lunch hours to continue our adventures.

One day I finally worked up my courage and asked, "Where did you folks come from, Johnny?"

Johnny paused a long time before answering. "We come over from the Rosebud Reservation the other side of the Missouri River. My old man come here to try to do some farmin'."

"Jeez, that's a long ways."

"We didn't go to school much over there," he continued. "School was far away, an' no good. My Ma got us some books to try to read. We ain't got nothin' but two more horses an' some rickety machinery," he said finally.

Freddie laughed. "That ain't no problem. You should see the shape our stuff is in. You'll be OK. The neighbors will help if you need some."

"We don't need no help," Johnny said sullenly.

"People around here help each other all the time," Freddie responded testily. He was getting impatient with Johnny's sullen pride.

"What's your Dad's name, anyway?" I asked to ease the tension.

"John Bear Day. People sometimes call him Chief."

"Jeez, is he a chief?"

"Naw, not really. He don't have no tribe to be Chief of."

"I'll bet he is one," I said. "Does that make you a Chief, too?"

Johnny Bear shook his head.

The social life at the school didn't go as well for Geneva. She didn't join in with the games. She would exchange a few words with Miss Bjerke, who was puzzled and frustrated in her efforts to reach her. Geneva appeared to be learning, but her unyielding reticence made it difficult to know if there was progress. Miss Bjerke finally decided to relax with her, treat her in a normal way, and hope she would gain confidence and learning from the schoolroom environment.

The other girls also gave up on Geneva, who was content to sit silently by herself during the recesses and lunch hours. One day, after some persistent prompting and prodding from the girls, Freddie Sanders decided to ask Johnny Bear about Geneva. "Why is she so quiet?

Why doesn't she want to have anythin' to do with the other kids?"

Johnny seemed reluctant to discuss it. He walked away, shaking his head slowly. Then he came back to us, looking down, kicking the dirt.

"It's pretty rough on the reservation sometimes," Johnny said. "Little kids sometimes get treated bad." He paused, and the other boys waited. "One time some older guys caught her alone and did something bad to her."

"Jeez, I know what that is," from Freddie, the wise one. "What did they do to the guys that done it?"

"Nothin'. There ain't much law on the reservation." Johnny spoke very softly, thinking about each word. "My old man did something to those guys, though. It was bad. There was a lot of bad things happened. That's why we left the reservation."

The subject was never mentioned among us boys again, and harking to some unspoken code, it was never mentioned to anyone else.

Freddie and I didn't find out much else about Johnny Bear's family, only bits of information he would mention from time to time. The family stayed at home, didn't mingle much with the community. Johnny told us one day that his grandfather was also called John Bear. They added the name Day to make them seem more "white," he said.

He never told us the name of his mother, only "my Ma," "Her," and "She." We found out eventually that her name was Bertha. She had once been Bertha Big Tree. She hardly ever left their bare, three bedroom house, and was never seen away from their farm.

There were only four of them, John Bear-Day, Bertha, Johnny Bear and Geneva. Johnny mentioned that he had older half-brothers and half-sisters, but they were never seen coming or going, and apparently never visited that house. John Bear got some Bureau of Indian Affairs welfare, and would scratch a skimpy living from his small, dry farm.

As spring wore on, Miss Bjerke was now hopeful that her little school would run smoothly until the summer break.

Then, one lunch hour, all five boys were busy near the road building a fort of willow branches, clay and dirt, and a few boards found in the barn. While we were busy concentrating on the job, a team of horses hauling a big grain wagon drew up and stopped on the road near the fort.

"Hey, it's Alfred and Orville," Freddie said. Alfred was an older boy, about 16, who lived in Verdon, the only town nearby. He was tough and mean. The other boy was Alfred's friend, equally nasty.

They climbed down from the wagon and came over to where we were standing. Slowly, deliberately they circled the fort and us boys. Then Alfred planted himself in front of us.

"Which one is that Indian kid?" he asked nastily. "As if I didn't know," he continued, stepping up close to Johnny Bear, bringing his face to within a foot of the smaller boy's.

"We don't want any Indian bucks hanging around here."

Johnny Bear stood silent. His eyes widened and there was a shadow of hurt on his face.

"I'm talkin' to you Redskin. You gonna leave this school?" He took another step toward the much smaller boy, nearly pushing him over, his fists clenched.

On a crazy impulse, I jumped between them, facing Alfred with my back to Johnny Bear.

"Leave him alone, he's OK," I said shakily.

Alfred's sneer twisted his face. "You little twerp. Who the hell you think you are? Get outa the way before I bust your teeth in."

Leon Krueger, even smaller than me, now also moved up beside me and Johnny Bear. Then Freddie joined us. The smaller boys stood in a close cluster.

"Are we goin' to hafta beat up on all you little jerks? That'll be fun!" Alfred turned to leer at the other big boy.

"Guess so," I said without conviction. Then Johnny Bear pushed me aside and stood up to the bully.

"Go ahead," he said.

Alfred swung hard at the boy's face, striking him just below the cheekbone. Johnny Bear went to his knees, but stayed upright. I watched, frozen, as he gasped for breath. Then Alfred drew back to strike him again just as Miss Bjerke stepped out on the porch, ringing the bell to call the children in to school. Orville saw her first.

"Let's go," he said to Alfred. "Here comes their Nanny Goat."

Alfred dropped his arm, unclenched his fist, and started backing toward the wagon. "You got away this time, Redskin, but we'll get you," and the two boys jumped on the wagon, slapped the horses with the reins, and started away.

Miss Bjerke watched them leave, then looked closely at Johnny Bear's cheek. She knelt to touch his face and try to comfort him. "Are you all right, Johnny?"

"I'm OK." He pulled away from her and stood, then wobbled to the schoolhouse, trying to conceal his dizziness, pain and embarrassment.

After school Johnny's cheek was swollen and sore. I thought he looked different now. The old hard edge had returned to his face, and his eyes were darker, and hurt. He didn't want to talk about it, but I did.

"Don't let 'em scare you off, Johnny," I pleaded. "We'll stand by you. Those guys aren't nothin'. Other folks don't feel that way. Those guys are just bullies lookin' for a fight. It don't mean nothin'. Don't let 'em chase you off, Johnny."

Johnny Bear looked out toward the horizon, toward where his family had come from. "I'm stayin'," he said.

Mister Brown

On a Saturday morning in the spring, he came trudging up the narrow road from the south, the flat fields stretching off to the horizon on both sides. My sister, Mary, was at the road by the mailbox and saw him first.

"Mama, Mama, Mister Brown is comin', he's walkin' up the road." She was running and jumping with excitement. She ran toward the house shouting in her squeaky voice.

The news quickly traveled through the house. Mother and the other girls rushed to the porch steps. It was a hot day in May and he looked wavy in the heat, kicking up puffs of dust as he strode along, a slowly growing, fuzzy apparition against the horizon.

"That old hobo, I didn't think he would show up again," Mother said. "What will we do with that old man?" She had come from the kitchen where she was fixing the noon meal, wiping her hands on her apron. She watched the man come slowly up the road, past the cattle pens, and turn into the house yard at the mailbox.

The children moved about restlessly, watching him approach. He was carrying a canvas bag about the size of a pillowcase over his shoulder. He came up to the cement apron extending out from the porch and wearily placed his bag down.

"Hullo, Missus," he said.

"Hello, Mister Brown."

"I come by box car as far as Conde," he said. "They only run that Northwestern train up this way once a week, so I hitch-hiked an' walked from Conde. Mostly walked. I finally got a ride part way, to the county line road."

"You hungry?"

"I ain't et much for a couple a days. I had some work down in Ioway, an' a lady give me a loaf of bread an' some meat. When that was gone I just kep' goin' to git here."

"Well, we will eat when Mr. Jones gets here in about half an hour. Why don't you go back to your old bunkhouse by the well and wash up? I don't know what condition that bunkhouse is in, you'll have to clean it out, I'm sure."

"I can do it, Missus."

He winked at me and touched his tattered felt hat. He was of medium build, slightly stooped. He wore a ragged denim jacket and cotton pants held up by wide elastic suspenders over a wrinkled, plaid cotton shirt. His face was coarse, with a wide nose, high cheekbones and a long, drooping mustache. He had a Slavic appearance, with a hint of American Indian. His face was deeply tanned, or wind-burned.

He hoisted up his sack, walked slowly around the corner of the house, and back toward the well and the bunkhouse at the edge of the small grove of stunted prairie trees. We children started to troop along with him, bursting with curiosity and questions.

"You children stay here," Mother said. "Just stay

here."

"Gee, Mama, why can't we go with Mister Brown?" Mary begged.

"You just can't, children. Not now. We'll talk about it this afternoon."

We continued to move about restlessly, occasionally peeking around the corner of the house toward the bunkhouse, then whispering to each other.

Finally, at noon, Dad came striding across the road from the barns.

Mary and I ran to the road to meet him. Mary was so excited about the visitor, the words came out in a single burst. "Mister Brown is here, Daddy. Brown's here. He just came walkin' up the road, Daddy. He looks real tired. Mama sent him to the old bunkhouse. Will he stay, Daddy?"

"Will you let him stay?" I asked.

He smiled at us and continued walking along the driveway to the house. He didn't say anything. We were craning our necks, trying to see his face, looking for a signal, waiting for him to speak.

"Can he stay, Daddy?" Mary asked again.

He cleared his throat and chuckled the quiet, gentle chuckle he reserved for us children.

"I'll have to talk to your Mother," he said.

Mary, who was the bravest of the children, said, "Daddy, sometimes you just say that, don't you? You don't always talk to Mama about all those things, do you?"

He smiled and continued up the driveway. Brown had seen us approaching the house, and was coming around the corner from the well when we reached the porch steps. He and Dad stood appraising each other.

"Hello, Brown," my Dad said.

"Hello, Mister." His great respect for our Dad

always showed when he spoke to him.

"Where have you been this time, Brown? Florida again?"

"Yeah. I was down that way — Arkansaw, Mississip', Alabam'. Got over to Floridy for awhile. Kep' movin' mosta' the time."

"Were you with the circus?" Dad let his glance stray toward us children. We held our breaths for his reply.

"I went down to Sarasoty and there-about, an' stayed around for a week or so, but they was full up. Didn't need no roust-abouts or animal feeders or cage cleaners. So I jist took off agin an' got a little work here an' there. Started workin' my way back north agin'."

Dad looked him over for awhile. We children were nearly motionless, waiting. Mother watched from the doorway.

Dad finally broke the silence. "How does that old bunkhouse look? I haven't been in there in months."

"She looks OK, Mister. Needs a little cleanin' out's all. Chickens been in there, an' lotsa mice."

Dad scraped his shoes on the iron scraper bolted to the doorstep. We waited.

"Well," he said finally. "Mrs. Jones will have something ready to eat pretty soon. We'll bring out a plate for you."

"All right, Mister. I'm beholdin' to you."

That was all that was ever said about employment and arrangements. Brown cleaned out the bunkhouse that afternoon. It was really a chicken house that had been converted to living quarters for the occasional hired hand. It was small, but reasonably tight to the weather, and dry. It was set under the gnarled prairie trees, and thus received additional protection.

MISTER BROWN

At supper, Mother put another plate of food on the back step. He took it to the bunkhouse and ate alone.

He was up the next morning at dawn, helping Dad with the chores and the milking, as if he had never been gone. He had never learned to drive a car or tractor, but was a magician in handling and managing animals.

"That old bum," Mother scolded. "That old transient. He's getting slower and slower. He's getting older and dirtier. Don't you children go near that bunkhouse."

But she knew we would flutter around him like moths as he did the chores around the place, asking him questions and listening raptly to his tales.

"Tell us about the circus, Mister Brown."

"What's it like in Alabam', Mister Brown? Are the children all black? Do they talk funny?"

Mother forbid us to ask more questions, and scolded Dad about it.

"Who knows what terrible trash he's telling those children. How can we have a dirty old man telling them all those tales? What will it do to the children? What a strange view they will have of the world!"

Dad grinned gently at her.

"He likes those children, Lydia. He's crazy about them. That's why he keeps coming back. I don't think he would do anything to hurt them."

"You don't think so? But what if he does?"

"He won't, Lydia."

"But you can't guarantee it?"

"No, I can't."

She went back into her kitchen muttering. I thought then she felt sorry for the old hobo, and that she liked him at least a little bit.

As the days and months of summer went by, it all came out. Bit by bit Brown would weave the tales for his rapt audience. About the hobos riding the trains.

About the men who chased them out of town. About how they sometimes got work, and sometimes begged for food. About soup lines, and biting dogs, and hobo camps on the edge of town.

We weren't allowed to go near the bunkhouse. Sometimes after he had finished his supper, he would sit for while on the steps of our house. Then we would gather around and ask him questions.

"What's it like riding in a box car, Mister Brown? Where do you sleep in the hobo camps? Do you cook over a fire? What do you cook?"

Brown would look in the door to see if Mother or Dad were going to call us inside or otherwise stop the conversation. If not, he would settle down, and we would stand or sit around him and wait.

"In Alabam', I fergit what town we was near, this lady come right into our hobo camp," he began. "She was dressed nice, with a big hat on, an' she was wavin' this bible an' talkin' to us. She wanted us to go with her to a church somewheres near.

"Nobody wanted to go with her. We was all dressed kinda rough an' dirty, so we didn't want to go into a church. Hobos ain't against religion, some of them has bibles an' prays a lot. But they is usually nervous around wimmin, specially church wimmin.

"This lady, she got about a dozen of the bo's to gather around one of the fires an' she prayed an' read from her bible an' sang some songs. We was polite to her but we didn't sing the songs like she wanted us to. Pretty soon she quit an' went off to go to church. The bo's just watched her go an' didn't say nothin' much about it."

"What about the circus, Mister Brown?"

"I wasn't down in Floridy very long this year," he began. "I come up on the old circus right in the same

MISTER BROWN

old place. Barnum and Bailey she was, biggest old circus in the whole world, she was. There she was, all unpacked off the trains and spread out to dry and rest up."

"Where were the animals, Mister Brown? Were they loose, or in cages, or what?"

"They puts the giraffes, buffaler, rhinos, all them animals that can't jump very high in a big pasture with a high, strong fence around it, and just let 'em roam. The big cats, gorillas, monkeys an' stuff they put in big cages on the ground, but they got a lot more room to move around than on the rail cars or in the circus tents. The elephants they keep chained up by the foot. They would jes' walk through any fence or bust up any cage."

"What do they feed 'em Mister Brown? Who feeds the animals?"

"Well, I still knowed a couple of fellers feedin' them animals. Guys I worked with a year or two past. They had a bunk tent right near the animals an' they let me stay there a couple of days, sleepin' on the straw and eatin' in their chow hall. Plenty of straw an' hay. I really slep' good. Lot bettern' a box car or a hobo jungle. Warm and dry there, but she sure smelled strong from them animals. Ya' get used to it, ya' do.

"What do they feed 'em? Well, them animals in the big pasture eat hay and grain. Just like them cattle there over the road. An' the cats and stuff, they eat some baled up discard from packing houses, and horse meat and stuff. It smells awful! I stay away from them cats and monkeys, and go by the animals that eats hay and grain. They smells a lot better, 'an they ain't as dangerous.

"I saw a guy get mauled up by one of them big cats. He was feedin' them an' he got careless. This one cat got him from the side, knocked him down an' started clawin' and bitin' him."

The children gasped. "Was he killed, Mister Brown? Did he die? Did the cat eat him?"

"Well, I hollered for help, an' grabbed a big iron bar that was layin' outside the door to the cage. I run in an' started hitting the cat on the head and shoulders. Some other guys was near by an' heard me holler an' him scream. They come runnin' over with some big clubs lying around the animal cages. They run in and started beatin' on the cat, too, an' he backed off, an' they drug the guy out of the pen. He was twitchin' and spurtin' blood. One guy started wrapping him up with some rags lyin' around an' the other ran to get the first aid guy.

"Both guys come back an' they started bandaging him up, and the ambulance came. I hear later he made it through OK."

"Boy, oh boy," I said. "He sure must have been scared. Weren't you scared, Mister Brown?"

"Well, I wasn't in much danger. There was other people on the way to help. But I was still scared for the guy."

"I'll bet he really had some awful scars," my sister Frances said. The others nodded and murmured assent.

"Did you see the trapeze people and the clowns and horse riders?"

"Yeah, I walked around and saw them people. They was practicin' an' talkin' an' workin' on their costumes an' their acts. They don't chase you away if you don't git in the way. Everything's kinda easy and slowed down. I been with them big circuses when they was on the road. Then its all hurry and rush, an' everybody shouting and cussin', an' going full speed, 'an sometimes there is some bad language."

MISTER BROWN

He would dip out a big chaw of Bull Durham tobacco from a pouch and roll it around in his mouth, get up and get the coffee can he used for a spittoon, even outdoors when he was near the house. We would wait while he settled himself back down. Then the questions would start again.

Mister Brown would go on and on in his gruff old man's voice with a Southern back-country twang to it.

"Three of us was walkin' around town in Jackson, Mississip' an' we saw three big white guys pickin' on a black man. They wasn't givin' him no chance to say nothin' or defend himself. They just kep' punchin' an' shovin' him an' accusin' him of stealin' some stuff from a store.

"The black guy, he didn't do nothin' to defend himself. Pretty soon they started hittin' him with their fists an' he finally went down. He still didn't do nothin' to defend himself except to try to protect his head an' face with his arms.

"The white guys was kickin' him when he was on the ground, and was hollerin' bad things at him. Pretty soon they got tired an' started to walk off. We was only about a half a block away an' they come over an' looked real mean at us, an' hollered at us, an' told us to get outa town or they'd see we was throwed in jail.

"When they was gone we went over to see if we could help the black guy. He was bleedin' quite a bit, but was able to get up when we helped him. He said he was OK, an' that he hadn't done nothin' wrong. He said if he had, they might've killed him He told us to keep out of it, an' he could make it home."

"Why were they so mean to the black man?" Ruth asked. "It wasn't fair what they did to him."

"Many of the whites in those Southern states are mean to the black people. It ain't fair 'cuz the blacks can't fight back. There's lotsa bullies among them whites in the South. Only thing I don't like about it."

Most of the stories were ordinary experiences to him, normal things that happen to a transient on the move. But to us, they were tales of distant and exciting places, of bizarre characters we would never expect to see or encounter on our everyday rounds of school, church and shopping.

"I come into Saint Joe, Missouri in a rainstorm," he began again, his voice soft and gruff as he remembered. "We was ridin' a Rock Island boxcar, me an' five other guys. We was all headin' north to look for jobs. There was a couple of kids, wasn't more than eighteen or nineteen years old. Then there was two guys goin' to Chicago, kep' pretty much to themselves. Just talked low to each other.

"Then there was this big guy, alone like me. He was pretty ragged, and looked kinda mean. He didn't say nothin' much, just sat with his back to the wall watchin' everybody.

"When the train slowed down outside Saint Joe, we all jumped off so we wouldn't run into any railroad cops, an' we walked up the tracks until we saw some smoke by the tracks, and there was some guys in a hobo camp. We found some shelter, and then them two guys from Chicago started cookin' some meat an' stuff they had brought with them. It really smelled good out there in the fresh air and rain.

"They was just startin' to eat when this big, mean guy comes over to them. He had about a three-foot piece of iron bar he had found somewhere, just swingin' from his right hand.

"'Gimme some 'a that stuff,' he said to them.

"The two guys looked at him, then looked at each other.

"'OK,' one guy says. 'Go ahead.' An' he gives him the pan.

"The big guy takes the pan, then puts down the iron bar to pick up a spoon, an' he starts to eat. Then the two guys from Chicago jumped him. One picks up the iron bar and pokes him hard in the stomach, then when he doubles over, starts hittin' him on the back and shoulders with it. He didn't hit him on the head, probably 'cause he might have killed him. The other one starts hittin' him with a home-made blackjack he had in his jacket.

"They didn't hurt him too bad. Maybe busted an arm an' put a few lumps on him, but they chased him outa the camp, an' we didn't see no more of him. It don't pay to be mean when you're on the road. It's better to just try to get along."

Mister Brown would rumble on about riding the rails, places he had been and characters with whom he had traveled, while the sun set and it began to grow dark. We children would move around him, now sitting beside him on the steps, now quietly walking back and forth, or standing close to not miss a word. We never interrupted, except to ask questions, for fear he would stop.

Then Mother would come to the doorway. "Time to wash up for bed, children," she would say softly.

Brown would get up from the step, slowly straightening his back, and groaning a little as he did so.

"G' night, Mister Brown."

"Good night, Mister Brown."

"G' night kids. See ya termorra," and off he'd go to his bunkhouse.

"I wonder if he really did all those things, Mama?" Frances asked. "Do you suppose he is making up some of that?"

"I don't really know, Frances. He's kind of a disreputable old bum, but I don't think he would lie to you children."

"I don't either," I said.

Brown always wore long underwear, summer and winter. He never seemed to be too warm, though in hot weather he smelled kind of strong. There was always one or more pair of long-handled underwear hanging from the short clothesline between the trees near his bunkhouse.

He always wore a flannel shirt. His concession to hot summer days was to turn up the sleeves of the shirt, leaving the gray-white long underwear sleeves extending down to his wrists. Brown said the long underwear kept him cool. He told our Dad he had tried wearing BVD's in hot weather, and said he got much more uncomfortable in the heat.

"Anyways, I only have one kind of underwear to worry about this way," he said.

One very hot day in late July, Mister Brown and I were making the long walk from the barns to the house for the noon-time meal. We had spent the morning shoveling and hauling grain to make room for the new crop. Actually, he had done most of the shoveling, and I had helped a little.

"Aren't you awful hot, Mister Brown?" I asked.

"Naw, not so bad. The sun feels kinda good."

"But you're just drippin' sweat!"

"Sweatin's good for you, boy. Gits all the pizen outa your body. I don't mind sweatin'. Been too many times when I was too cold. I got to kind of store up some heat for them cold winter days on the road."

"You goin' away again this winter?" I wanted to know.

"Well, I guess so. I gets lonesome for them palm

trees and hobo camps down south."

"Do you have friends and family down there?"

"Naw, I don't have nobody at all. You're my family." He looked at me and grinned.

The work became very heavy that fall. Our Dad had taken on more land. There was more harvesting, fall plowing and livestock to look after. Brown told Dad he would stay through Christmas before heading south.

On a Saturday before Christmas, Dad and Mother decided to leave us at home for a few hours and go to Groton to do some Christmas shopping. It was a clear, cold, sunny day, and they would be only twelve miles away. They told Ruth, the eldest, she was in charge of the house, and of the rest of us. A big responsibility for a twelve-year-old.

Just before noon, Mister Brown and I were carrying feed to the milking cow's yard when he noticed a low, dark cloud rolling and roiling rapidly toward us from the northwest. Brown had seen powerful prairie storms before. "This is a bad one," he said to me.

We rushed to herd the animals into the yards and buildings. In less than ten minutes, the blizzard struck with crushing, breath-taking force, a sweeping, seemingly solid wall of dust and dirt thrown up by the rising wind, followed immediately by heavy, stinging snow. The buildings, fences, animals all disappeared into the swirling, driving storm. Brown kept me close, then hung onto me as we groped around the barnyard, trying to get the animals reasonably protected. Then we began to worry about the girls in the house, and how to get there.

Our barns were more than 300 yards from the house, with a fence and a road about halfway between. We started in what we hoped was the direction of the house, but after many minutes we hadn't run into the fence or the road, and began to worry. I was beginning to feel frozen. I tried not to cry, but for a six-year-old who thought he was freezing to death, that wasn't so easy. I just hung on to Mister Brown's jacket sleeve.

He adjusted his direction and kept going. Neither of us had dressed for a brutal, sub-zero blizzard. I could feel my face was already frozen, and my arms and legs were beginning to feel numb and lifeless. The wind was tearing at our clothing. We could barely keep our eyes open in the pounding maelstrom.

After ten more minutes of panicky groping through the storm, we ran into the fence. We followed it one way, then the other until we found the gate to mark the place where we should cross the road. We had used up another ten minutes finding the gate, and I was sure I was freezing. Mister Brown's hands couldn't close to grasp the wires and open the gate. He smashed it with his foot, and it sprung open. Another ten minutes of slowly, desperately stumbling and groping and we ran into the grove where the bunkhouse stood. From there we painfully made our way to the house to join my frightened sisters.

At the same time in Groton, Dad and Mother stepped out of Miller's Store to confront the blinding, smothering blizzard. Later they told us all about it. They couldn't see across the street or even breathe in the blizzard. They couldn't even consider trying to get home. The blinding blizzard went on until well after dark, when the wind finally died down enough so they could see a few feet.

Mother told us they were sick with worry about us. The telephone lines went down when the storm hit. She said she was worried about Mister Brown. Whether he would take care of us. Whether he might harm my sisters.

MISTER BROWN

At daylight they started out, bucking drifts, following the plows, pushing and shoveling. It was mid-afternoon when Mother and Dad finally smashed through the last high drifts and turned into our yard. We had been watching for them, and met them at the doorstep. After hugs all around, Mother looked at us closely. Mister Brown was in the other room, adding wood to the fire in the kitchen stove.

"Are you children all right?" she asked.

"We're fine, Mama, just fine," Ruth said. "Mister Brown has been keeping the fires going and fixed us some food. I helped him. Frances and Mary did the dishes and made the beds, and Howard and Mister Brown dug us out this morning and shoveled a path so we could get more wood."

"You all right, Brown?" Dad asked.

"I'm OK. It was kinda scary when the blizzard was goin' hard an' I didn't know for sure whether Howard and I could find the house. But we did. It was terrible cold. I never been so cold. Thought we was freezin' to death. I woulda just give up, but had to keep goin' cuz those girls in the house might be in trouble. Now I gotta git out there an' dig out some feed for them animals."

"Stay here in the kitchen and keep warm, and nurse that frostbite," Dad said. "I'll look after the livestock."

"Naw. I'm OK. Let's go do it."

"OK, partner," Dad said.

Mother stopped Brown at the door with a hand on his arm. It was the first time she had ever touched him. "Thank you, Brown, for looking after the children. Thank you so much." Her eyes flooded with tears.

"Aw, Missus, that was nothin'. I'd do anything for them kids. You know that."

"I know now," she said.

The Horses

John Bear Day, Johnny and Geneva's father, had begun to be seen more often in the neighborhood. He was a rugged, sturdy man in worn work clothes. He had straight, jet-black hair cut long by his wife, typical high cheekbones, weathered lines and wrinkles, dark eyes and a ready smile.

The neighbors liked him when they ran into him at the tiny country store in Verdon, or occasionally on the road or in the fields. The conversations were brief and uninspired. Just a greeting, a few words about the weather and the crops, and a wave goodbye. Nobody ever saw his wife.

John Bear was becoming interested in the school. He was thrilled to see his children learning, to hear them talk about their lessons, and about the other children and the teacher. Johnny told Freddie and me about his Dad's interest in the school. He had been in a reservation school for only a few scattered months when he was a young boy. He could read, write and do simple mathematics. He had a lively, inquiring mind, and read everything that came within his reach, including Johnny's and Geneva's schoolbooks.

He would walk, or drive his horses and wagon

past the schoolhouse on his regular rounds of working and managing his farm, and he would think warmly about the wonders his children were learning in there.

One day as he drove by, it was the lunch hour. We children had eaten and were playing in the schoolyard. Miss Bjerke had come out on the porch to enjoy a few minutes of fresh air and sunshine. On impulse, John Bear stopped his rig, climbed down and approached the porch.

"Hullo, M'am. I'm John Bear Day, Johnny and Geneva's dad."

"How do you do. I'm Minnie Bjerke."

There was a pause. John Bear was embarrassed. The children in the yard were silent, watching. His son and daughter had faded into the background.

"They're doing fine, Mr. Bear. Johnny is a good student. He is learning steadily, right along with the other children. Geneva is very shy, but we get along." She smiled. "She's learning."

He nodded, still shy. "I know they are learnin'. It is really great how good they are gettin' along. I really want to thank you."

"Well, that's nice, but it isn't necessary. I'm here to help the children learn, and I enjoy it."

"Anyway, their Ma and I are beholdin' to you. Neither of us got much education, so we really like to see our kids learnin'. You just let me know if there is anything I can do."

He turned to leave, and on impulse Miss Bjerke said, "There is something you can do."

John Bear turned back with a look of surprise and pleasure. "What can I do, M'am?"

Now that she had gotten herself into the situation, Miss Bjerke lost some of her usual self-assurance.

"Well, I'd like to have the children know more

about your people. You know." She paused.

"You mean tell 'em about Indians?" he asked.

"Well, yes, as part of our history and geography. Johnny has mentioned that you come from an interesting background."

He grinned. "Johnny must be braggin'. Our background was generally pretty bad."

"He just mentioned that your father and grandfather were also John Bear."

"Well, somethin' like that."

"Would you tell us about it some day? Maybe just come for an hour and let the children ask questions. Or you could tell them some history of your people."

"Some of it ain't so good, M'am."

"I know that. You could decide what to tell."

"I don't talk so good, you know."

"Well, I don't think that's so important. It's what you have to tell us that counts. I'm sure the children would like it very much."

"I'll think about it. Gimme a few days to think about it."

A few days later Johnny reluctantly brought the word from home. "My Old Man says he will talk to the kids. If you want, he will come next Monday after noon-hour."

"Why, that's wonderful, Johnny. We are all looking forward to it."

Johnny seemed very glum about the situation. He told Freddie and me he had begged his father not to do it, but John Bear was adamant. "She asked me to do it, an' I'm gonna do it. I ain't goin' back on my word." And that was that.

On Monday afternoon, he came to the school as promised. "Can we do this on the porch, M'am?

I feel better outside."

"Certainly. The children will enjoy that. We'll gather around. It's a beautiful day."

We were thrilled to be out of the schoolhouse and into a holiday, story-telling mode — except for Johnny and Geneva, who stayed back as far from their father as possible.

John Bear Day sat with his back to the schoolhouse wall, with the children and teacher arranged around him on the porch and on the ground. The northwest breeze brought soft, earthy smells off the spring prairie and an occasional wisp of dust. He spoke slowly, using the best English and grammar he could muster.

"My Pa was called John Bear," he began. "He wasn't much account. Just stayed on the reservation near Rosebud. I remember his Pa, who would have been my Grandpa. He had an Indian name, but was sometimes called John Bear, too. Then I used to hear about an old, old man, long before him, who was a real Indian." He grinned. "They called him Running Bear.

"We didn't always stick to families 'an family lines as much as other people do. There was just kind of a long line-up of men and women who go way back together, who stayed together and made a close bunch. Years ago they called them bands, sometimes tribes. People would mix back and forth between the bands, but mostly they'd hang together around a head man, who would pass it along to another head man, what some people call "Chiefs."

"The head men were leaders because they was the smartest or strongest. It wasn't like no king, or anything like that. Them chiefs had to look out for themselves, just like everybody else.

"There was a lot of story telling around the camps. When we was kids, we'd hang around the shacks or tipis, as close as we could get to a warm fire, and listen to the stories those old guys would tell. The women knew a lot, too. They really told more about the old days than the men did. They was kind of the keepers of the stuff about the old times. The men told more about fightin' and huntin'.

"My Grandpa told a story about how our people first got some horses."

"Gosh," Freddie exclaimed, "you mean there was a time when Indians didn't have horses? Where were the horses?"

"Well, there just wasn't any where my people come from. They didn't find no horses until later. In the early days they just walked. After they got horses things got a lot easier.

"Them people, in the times before my Grandpa, was driven out of Canada and Minnesota by some big, tough tribes over there. They had a big battle up in Canada, in a place called Sioux Narrows, and got chased away. They finally stopped runnin' and settled down and was camped around the lakes in them low hills east of here. You can see them hills from here," and he pointed to the profile of the Antelope Moraines to the east. "That was long before them tame Sioux came over here from Minnesota.

"They would come down into this valley and plain, an' hunt buffalo. Then they would carry the meat back to the camps in the hills an' spend the winter there."

"You mean they hunted buffalo right here where we are?" Phyllis asked.

"Well, they probably did. This land once had big buffalo herds."

The children looked around them at the open prairie, then at each other.

"I think he's right," Miss Bjerke said.

THE HORSES

John Bear nodded to her, then continued. "One fall, after the hunt, while the buffalo was being butchered by the women, some of the hunters decided to travel ten days to the west to see what was out there. They crossed the Jim River and on the seventh day they come to the Missouri River. It was so shallow they crossed it on sand bars, an' when they come up on the far side they saw a great, big flat land, waving with short grass that went as far as they could see.

"They went on for two more days, seein' big herds of buffalo an' smaller herds of antelope, an' then they saw the people with the horses. They hadn't never seen horses before, but they had heard about them. They was big, could carry a man on their backs easy. Some was brown, some was spotted. They looked like they could run fast.

"There was eight hunters in the other group, each ridin' one of them horses single file across that flat grassland. The riders didn't see our scouts, who dropped into the deep grass watchin' 'em. Our people was shakin' with excitement, but afraid to even breathe for fear of bein' discovered an' run over by them people on their big animals.

"They watched them disappear over the horizon. They knew right then they would have to have horses, then life would be better. After the Cheyenne disappeared, they started back to the hunters' camp, an' when they got there they told the band about what they seen. They helped move the meat an' hides back to the main camp. It was snowin' when the last loads was carried more than thirty miles from the hunter's camp to the main camp up by the lakes.

"The band spent the winter fixin' up their camp, curin' the hides, makin' warm clothes from the thick skins, passin' it around so everybody got enough meat an' some hides. All winter the talk was about what the hunters had seen out west, an' specially 'bout the horses. The hunters had to tell the story over and over about the buffalo, the antelope an' the horses.

"Durin' the winter they agreed on a plan for the next year. They would have a spring buffalo hunt to build up their meat supply an' get more hides for clothes an' shelter. Then a small huntin' party of their best men would set out to try to find and capture some horses."

John Bear stopped. "Am I goin' along all right?" he asked Miss Bjerke.

She looked at the children.

"Oh boy, we want to hear about the horses!" Leon Krueger spoke up.

"Yeah, you can't stop now! We want to hear the rest of the story."

"We should let Mr. Bear go back to his work if he needs to," Miss Bjerke said.

"Ain't he goin' to finish the story?" Freddie asked.

John Bear grinned. "I guess I better keep goin'." He stretched his legs, and shifted his position with his back against the schoolhouse wall.

"The next spring, after the early hunt was over, seven men went west to try to find and capture some horses. "Ol' John Bear was leader of the party. They crossed the Jim and Missouri Rivers agin'. Probably passed right near here. They saw thousands of buffalo an' nearly as many of them fast antelope. They finally reached a beautiful area of high hills and pine trees, an' searched there for the people with the ridin' animals and found nothin'. They were killin' a small animal or a buffalo once in awhile, and livin' off the land.

"From the Black Hills they went south, plannin' to make a big circle, travelin' south, then east, and finally north back to their home camp. They went south an' east until they come to a wide, almost dry river. They followed the riverbed east for a day, then suddenly come upon a big camp of the other people. Near the camp was a herd of the ridin' animals, dozens of 'em. Them braves of ours was struck dumb, an' threw themselves down outa sight an' wondered what to do.

"Slowly they drew back from the camp. When they were a mile away, behind a small bluff, they gathered for a council. They figured the people were Cheyennes, who some of them had heard about.

"Over the years there was a lot of different stories about what happened next. It went somethin' like this: They talked about how to get them horses, an' Runnin' Bear finally decided what they would do. He and two other hunters would hide near the camp and learn how them Cheyenne handled the horses. He told the others to wait three days an' if they didn't return, the other four would have to go in an' try to get some horses as best they could. He told them that any who got captured prob'ly would be tortured and killed by the Cheyenne.

"The three that went in to watch hid themselves good. For two nights an' two days they watched the camp, studied how the Cheyenne worked them horses. They saw how they caught them, hobbled them, mounted and rode them. They watched what they did over and over, until they was sure they knew how to do it, an' how to tell the others.

"The third night they returned to the other four. They slept, then the next day went over and over exactly how they would capture and handle the horses, and how they would get away. Every little thing about how to find and use the leathers for controlling the animals, how to knot the thongs around the lower jaw, how to use it to guide the runnin' horse, how to get on the horse, an' how to stay there.

"It was a dangerous raid. They had to surprise the Cheyenne, steal the horses, learn to handle 'em, then get away fast enough to keep from gettin' captured and killed. They was sick with fear. They was also brave. They knew some of 'em would be killed.

"Each man was goin' to try to capture an' escape with a horse. So as not to lead the pursuing Cheyenne back to their home camp, they would run northwest, toward the Black Hills. Them who was not killed or captured would hide near a river crossing they all remembered, three days to the northwest. The run to the meetin' place would require two days with horses, four or more days crawlin', or draggin' wounded. Those who reached the crossing would wait through the fifth day, then start on a straight line for the home camp.

"When it was fully dark, they started crawlin' up to the horse herd. Soon they was near enough to hear the sounds of the camp slowin' down, an' then the Cheyenne began to sleep. They inched around to the side of the camp near where the horse herd had been brought in close and hobbled for the night. They could hear the animals snortin' and stampin', even hear their tails switchin' at the flies.

"They waited. In the dark, away from the dyin' campfires, they had the seein' advantage. The Cheyenne runnin' from the light into the dark, would be blinded 'til their eyes adjusted. That, an' surprise, would be their advantage.

"They crawled closer. Runnin' Bear showed them where there was leather thongs used to steer and lead the animals. One man went in slowly to get some of the leathers, givin' them another advantage in speed of the raid. Some of the horses raised their heads and stamped as he moved past them.

"But they was used to men movin' among them. They didn't send out no alarm. He come back with the leather strips. It was a great piece of luck. In the dark, each man tried to pick out the horse he would try to capture.

"The time had come. Runnin' Bear looked at each man, then whispered 'go.'

"The Cheyenne village was quiet. The raiders moved forward, an' then they was among the hobbled horses. The next five minutes was a wild scramble.

"One man just moved up quietly to a tremblin' horse, slipped the leather over its lower jaw, untied the hobble strips, an' led 'im away.

"Another man had picked a mean, spooky animal. When he touched it, it began to snort and plunge, screamin' like an animal under attack. The horse reared an' slashed at 'im with its hooves, an' he went down, bleedin an' unconscious.

"When that crazy horse exploded, the whole herd began to plunge and holler. There was shouts and runnin' in the Cheyenne camp.

"Runnin' Bear got his rawhide around a horse's jaw, an' dragged the scared horse away from the herd and toward the northwest. He was trampled and bruised, an' had a broken ankle, but he kep' movin' as best as he could.

"Another man had picked a gentle mare. He looped his leather thong under her jaw, jumped on her back, an' guided her in a crazy gallop away from the camp, hangin' onto her mane with both hands.

"The rest of 'em was lost in the mess of snortin' animals, shoutin' Cheyenne, an' screamin' women an' children.

"Each of the three guys who got away traveled

northwest, always lookin' back for pursuit. Bear, with the damaged ankle, after an hour of great pain, decided to try to ride his horse. Over the next hour he fell off or was throwed off many times. He hung on to the jaw thong, an' the horse did not get away. Anythin' was better than walking on the busted ankle.

"The first man to get his horse out led it at a run, hour after hour, sometimes falling in the dark, but never letting go of his horse. At dawn he could not see any pursuit so he slowed to a fast, steady walk.

"One of our guys missed capturing a horse an' just run north and west when the horse herd went wild. At dawn he buried himself deep in a willow an' grass cluster beside a small stream. He lay there all day, an' that night started on a direct line toward the meetin' place at the stream crossing.

"The two hunters who was ridin' saw each other first, a day's ride short of the stream crossing. They finished the trip, found the exact place, an' hid themselves and their horses a half-mile away, so they could watch for the other raiders or for pursuit. The next day the raider leadin' his horse came into the area. The fourth day the fourth man, walkin' alone, showed up.

"He told the other three that he had seen two of the hunters killed or wounded by the Cheyenne. He didn't see anybody else get away from the horse herd. He was ashamed that he hadn't captured a horse, an' was silent through all the days back to the home camp."

"How come the Cheyenne didn't chase them?" Freddie broke the rapt silence.

"Well, our people thought maybe it was because they didn't expect no raid from the northwest. There wasn't no Indians up that way at that time. They probably was lookin' to the south and east. Also, they was probably busy torturin' the ones that got caught, if they was still alive.

"Anyways, on the sixth day after the raid, they hadn't seen anything of the other three. They was worried that the Cheyenne might find 'em, wipe 'em out, an' take back the horses. They had waited longer than they had agreed to wait. They felt bad about the guys who got killed or tortured, but the life of a hunter was pretty dangerous, an' gettin' killed was part of it.

"Soon after dawn, with Runnin' Bear who had the bad ankle ridin', an' the other three walkin' and leadin' the horses, they started their long trip home.

"The horses they had stole were a sorrel, a black 'n bay, an' a brown an' white pinto. They happened to be a stallion an' two mares. They had the stock for raisin' their own horse herd for huntin', carryin' an' raids.

"Over the years they raised foals an' stole more horses. As the number of animals they had grew, so did their good livin'. From the lake camp in the hills there came bands of families movin' west, out across the Missouri to the Black Hills, an' beyond to the rivers an' valleys on the east side of the Rocky Mountains.

"Them Dakota Sioux became a great nation of hunters an' warriors, thanks to their growin' herds of horses. They was known as the 'Horse Indians' an' for awhile our people was number one on the plains of Dakota, Montana an' Wyoming, chasing away or killing other peoples who wanted to move into our territory.

"Then came the first white men, then the soldiers. In a few years our people lost almost the whole thing. They fought hard, won some battles with the whites, but was finally defeated, betrayed and murdered. But, some of 'em hung on. We're still here."

He grinned at the children and, groaning a little,

stood up on the porch. "Well, I guess I wore out you kids with too much story tellin'."

Miss Bjerke broke in. "It was an exciting story. We are so grateful to you."

"Boy, that was a great story. You goin' to tell us some more stuff about the old days?" I asked.

"I'll come back agin' sometime if Miss Bjerke wants me to."

"Of course we do," she said.

Johnny and Geneva moved closer to their father, and grinned at the other kids.

The Well

The earth warmed, and the smell of the rich soil and of the tiny green plants thrusting up into the sunlight was carried through the open schoolroom windows. We all grew more restless as the days got warmer. Johnny Bear, Freddie and me had to force ourselves to enter the gloom of the tiny school.

Then the warm days turned hot, the gentle spring rains stopped, and easterly winds swung around to the south, searing and dry. Summer arrived, and school was dismissed until fall.

Suddenly we were free, but separated.

I had plenty of work to do around the farm. I was up early to help with feeding the animals. I had started to drive the tractor and trucks, although I was barely big enough to reach the controls. I followed my Dad and Mister Brown day after day, doing what I was told. The days passed quickly, but I missed my school friends. I was lonesome for the schoolyard conversations with boys my own age, and the fun things we had done together.

As the summer progressed, the rains stayed away and the temperature soared. The wheat plants shriveled, the stunted corn stalks curled in the heat, then started to turn brown months ahead of their natural schedule. The livestock began to roam the pastures bawling their hunger, desperately searching for some greenery to nibble on.

In late July I got word to Freddie and Johnny Bear by way of Richie Miller, the mailman, to come over on a Saturday afternoon to exchange news and stories about the summer, and to splash in the cool water in the big stock watering basin fed by our deep artesian well.

Johnny Bear left his home after lunch on the pinto pony, picking up Freddie to ride double for the last two miles. When they arrived at our place, there were big hellos and shouts of laughter. We grinned and grinned at each other, cuffed each other on the arms and chests, and collapsed on the ground in a weak, friendly, three-way wrestling match.

After five minutes of horsing around, we were sweating and dirty, but happy.

"Let's go to the well and cool off," I suggested.

Our well was supposed to be about 1200 feet deep. Just a four-inch pipe, encasing a hole drilled straight down through the gumbo and shale and other strata, into the porous layer more than a thousand feel below. Then a smaller pipe with a three-foot perforated section at the bottom was lowered inside the casing, and the flow of water miraculously began,

The water gathered in the basin formed at the foot of the casing deep in the earth, had filtered down from the Coteau des Prairies, sometimes called the Antelope Moraines — hills that rose slowly out of the flat prairie, finally reaching nearly 1200 feet at its ridges twenty miles to the east. The ever-flowing artesian wells were the remarkable, life-giving miracle on that flat, dry prairie.

Our well ran steadily and strongly year after year.

THE WELL

Once the collecting basin had formed at the lower end of the well casing, and the roiling sand and other aggregate had settled down, the well was never shut down.

My Dad had told us that if we turned off the well, shut it down completely, the water in the pool way down below would become turbulent and muddy. It would spoil the well for awhile, maybe even plug it up for good. Then the cool, clean water would never run again, and the cattle and horses, and the family, would be without water in the searing heat of the windy summer until another well could be dug, which would take weeks of work and waiting, and cost money we didn't have.

The thin stream of water from the ever-flowing artesian well was our fountain of life. We knew the creeks and the James River were dry. The Missouri River was more than 100 miles away, and probably dry, also. The artesian wells were the only source of water on that endless, parched prairie that summer of 1934. The wells kept the cattle, horses and chickens alive, and the animals and fowls kept the families alive. Without water, nothing would survive for long.

At the well, we turned on the standpipe faucet and began to splash in the pool being formed below the faucet. As the pool was enlarged by the running water, we took off our shoes and shirts to better enjoy the coolness of the clear water. Soon we were dripping wet and smeared with mud.

After awhile we got bored with just splashing and soaking each other, and got to talking about the well.

"What did your Pa say would happen if you shut off the well?" Freddie asked.

"He said it would get all stirred up an' maybe plug itself up."

"I wonder if it really would," Freddie mused.

"I don't think we ought to fool with it," Johnny

Bear said.

"Me neither," I shook my head.

Freddie was looking for some excitement. "I don't know if it would be so bad. My Pa has never said nothin' like that 'bout our well. Probably your Pa just didn't want you foolin' with it."

I was scared. "Boy, I'd be scared to try anything. We could get into bad trouble."

"Let's leave it alone. We don't want no trouble. We're havin' a good time. Let's go over to the stock pond and wade around." Johnny Bear started to walk away.

"You guys are really scaredy cats," Freddie taunted. "You're like a couple 'a girls. I never knew you was such chickens."

"I guess I'm scared, all right," I said. "If we ruined that well, it would be really bad around here."

"Aw, you ain't goin' to ruin the well. That's just grown-up talk to scare us. I dare you to turn it off. I dare you, Howard, you scaredy cat. You're not that chicken are you, Howard?"

"Don't let him talk you into it," Johnny Bear warned.

"C'mon, Howard, I dare you. C'mon. Turn it off an' we'll count one hundred and turn it on again. That ain't nothin'. Even a scaredy girl like you could do that!"

One valve on the standpipe was for the long pipe that ran to the cattle yards, more than 300 yards away. It was never turned off. The over-flow from the stock watering tank flowed into the stock pond, where it evaporated back into the air. The second valve regulated the flow of water to the house. Then there was the faucet for taking water at the well-head, where we stood.

I was frozen in indecision for a moment, while the two other boys watched me. Then I stepped up to

THE WELL

the well and turned both valves and the faucet shut. The well was closed down.

Johnny Bear shook his head and walked away.

Freddie stood watching, counting. "Twenty-four, twenty-five, twenty-six..."

I was again frozen, looking at the valves, then at the silent puddle beneath the well faucet. The enormity of what I had done finally hit me. Not only had I turned off the well and endangered the whole farm, but I had gone against my Dad's word. That had never happened before. I dropped to my knees and stared at the well pipe, my mouth open, my jaw hanging loose.

Freddie was counting. "Sixty-seven, sixty-eight, sixty-nine..."

"Jeez, Freddie, we shouldn't 'a done it. Oh my God!" I groaned.

"Oh, shut up, or you'll make me lose count! Eighty-three, eighty-four, eighty-five..."

I was up now, nervously fidgeting around the valves, looking at Freddie, watching him count.

"Ninety-seven, ninety-eight, ninety-nine, one hundred. Turn 'em on Howard!"

I opened the well-head faucet first, not daring to send what might be coming up from the well to the house or the barns.

We watched with horror as the well ran clear for a few seconds, then spewed filth. Mud and sand in ugly, watery globs streamed out to spoil the pool at the base of the standpipe.

"My gosh, Freddie, what'll we do? Lookit that yukky stuff! What if my Mom or Dad come over here? We'll be killed!"

Freddie, the cool one, stood firm, watching the ugly, dirty water flow from the faucet. "We got to wait a minute. It ain't plugged up. It's still running.

Maybe it'll get better."

We waited, periodically glancing over our shoulders toward the house and barns where one or the other of my parents might be.

"It's beginnin' to clear up a little, I think." My voice was hoarse and shaky.

Just then my Mother stepped out of the house and called to us. "What's wrong with the well, boys? There's no water in the house."

I was mute, trying not to look at the muddy, running water. Mother quickly strode to where we were standing. Freddie looked around and decided it was too late to run. Johnny Bear was already standing a ways away, separating himself from the activity at the wellhead.

"What's wrong? It's all muddy." Her eyes widened as she realized what must have happened. "Oh, no!" she gasped. Then her voice dropped to a quiet, deadly tone. "Who turned off the well, boys?"

Nobody spoke.

"Howard?"

I was mute, frozen again.

"Freddie?"

Freddie just looked at the well, and shook his head.

"Johnny?"

"No, Missus, not me," he said.

Mother turned back to the well where Freddie and I were concentrating on the dirty water spewing from it. She stood for several silent seconds, looking from one of us to the other, then to the well.

I couldn't stand it any longer. "Please don't tell Dad, Mom," I pleaded. "Just don't tell him."

She looked at me with astonishment. "Don't tell Daddy? You may have destroyed us all. Everything we have. Everything your Father and I have worked

THE WELL

for —" Her voice broke in a half-sob.

She recovered her composure and turned squarely to me. "Go in and look after Helen," she ordered. "I must go and see your Father." She strode rapidly toward the barns.

"I think we'd better go," Freddie said. "We got to get home before supper. Let's go, Johnny."

Johnny Bear went slowly toward where the pinto was tied to a tree branch, and brought him to the well. The horse sniffed the water in the pool beneath the faucet and backed away.

"I'm really sorry, Howard." Johnny Bear grabbed the horse's mane and jumped lightly aboard.

"Let's go," Freddie urged him, climbing up behind him. "Let's get outa here."

I watched them kick the horse into a canter and pass quickly out of the yard and down the road. Then I went into the house as ordered.

In half an hour my Dad came quickly to the well. I watched him go past the house, his face more stern and grim than I had ever seen it. He glanced briefly at me in the doorway, then carefully at the water running from the faucet on the well. It was beginning to clear. He tasted it, then spit it out.

He looked at me a long time. I had left the house and was standing nearby. My Dad's face held an inquiring, sad look I had never seen before.

Finally, he spoke. "Go inside, Howard."

I was shaking so I could hardly walk. My knees and legs felt rubbery and weak as I retreated toward the house.

Dad continued to watch the water for a short time, looked across the fields to the horizon, no doubt recalling the years of back-breaking work and struggle to bring their venture this far, then turned away. He stopped at the house, spoke briefly to Mother, then continued on to his work in the barnyards. Neither of them spoke to me.

Later, supper was grim and silent. All of the children were drawn and subdued, seldom looking up from their plates. We all felt the terrible tension and concern.

After supper, Dad went out to the well, stayed awhile, then returned to the kitchen. My sisters were helping clear up after the meal, stacking the dishes in the sink until the water cleared. I was trying to be as out-of-sight as possible. Dad stood inside the kitchen door.

"You made a terrible mistake, Howard." His voice was low, but with a hard edge I had never heard before. Not kindly and teasing as it usually was with us children.

"The well probably will recover," he said. "It may never be as good as it was before. I hope you never do anything that irresponsible again. You not only endangered the animals and your home, but you actually threatened our lives. Your Mother and I are very disappointed in you. We didn't believe you could do such a thoughtless thing."

He turned and left the kitchen, striding out into the twilight to finish his work with the animals. Nothing more was ever said to me by my Mother or Dad about the incident with the well. It would continue to supply us will clear, cool water, endure and survive, and so would we. But I carry a scar that never faded away

The Hunters

After hearing John Bear's story about the horses, the curiosity about the Bear-Day family and the Indian history of the Northern Dakotas was a hot subject in the neighborhood. The children took the story home, of course, re-told with great enthusiasm and inaccuracy.

At school the children begged Miss Bjerke for another story session with Mr. Bear-Day. She finally asked Geneva and Johnny to speak to their father. A few weeks later he showed up at the school and took his place on the porch with the children gathered around.

"This story maybe ain't as exciting as the horse story," he said. "It's been passed down by my people for many generations.

"My granny used to sit at the fire back on the Rosebud Reservation and tell stories about the old times," he said. "She said our people once lived in a land filled with cool, blue lakes and tall pine trees. She said my great-great-grandfather and many others had been killed in a battle with the strong tribes from the North and East when the people had fought to hold them back at a place between two beautiful lakes far to the north, now called Sioux Narrows.

"They had lost a big fight with the Crees, and another with the Chippewa and had retreated away from that land of deer, moose, bear and fish. On foot they wandered west and south, lookin' for a place to hunt and live.

"They stopped one winter at them two big inland lakes, the Red Lakes, and filled up on fish. But, their enemies chased them and they went on past many smaller, beautiful lakes, keepin' westward, headin' south toward warmer weather. The thick, tall pine trees gave way to more open ground — rolling meadows and then a flat, deep-grass valley.

"They was afraid when the pine forests and lakes give way to open, rolling land, but more afraid to stop and risk being killed by them hostile tribes. Their number was getting smaller as the old people began to give up and die, and many of the usual sick and wounded did not recover because of their steady move west.

"During their first winter on the open land away from the lakes and pines, they suffered bad from starvation and cold. There was no large animals to hunt for meat and skins. No fish. The rickety shambles of their woodland shelters that they had been draggin' along weren't sturdy enough or thick enough to withstand the winter blizzards an' cold they faced on the open land. They lost more women and children, and some men, and most of their old people that first winter on the flatland.

"The younger, strong ones went out hunting to bring back a few rabbits, some foxes, badgers and other small animals. It wasn't enough, and the band grew weaker.

"By spring they was discouraged and didn't know what to do. They wondered should they return, in their weakened condition to the East and try to force a place for themselves among the strong tribes that had driven them away? Was death by battle for the men and slavery for their women and children worse than starving and freezing out on them open, empty plains?

"As the snow began to melt and the land began to turn green, they argued, with no decision.

"Finally, Running Bear said, 'I will take my lodge and people toward the sunset one more summer, looking for a better place, a place with bigger animals we can kill and eat, and skins we can use for clothing and shelter. If we find nothing, we may die before we can return, but we will go. If any of you want to join us you are welcome. We will leave at the second sun.'

"On the second morning, as the sun rose, the whole camp was up and movin' about, takin' down the rickety shelters, makin' them into packs to carry, or to drag on sticks. What little dried food they had was carefully wrapped in skins and carried by trusted grown-ups. There was less than two hundred people left in the ragged caravan slowly dragging itself away from the familiar lands. The younger men ranged out to left and right and front, watching for game and danger.

"The third day they reached the River That Runs North, just clearing of winter ice and runnin' over it's banks. Rather than cross it there, they decided to follow it south toward its source, searching for a better place to cross. The hunters was findin' and killin' a few small animals, enough to keep the band from starvin', not enough to satisfy its hunger, or to keep the few little ones who had survived the winter from cryin'. They hunted hard an' long, then one day the hunter far out in front come upon the headwaters of the River That Runs North, a long, narrow lake.

"It was not round and deep like the lakes they knew. It was shallow, narrow and muddy. There was no pine trees, only low willows and scrub trees, still without leaves. But it was a lake, deeper water, and there should be fish. They knew how to catch fish, and they began to catch 'em. Finally, there was a feast. The half-cleaned, half-cooked fish were wolfed down as fast as they caught 'em. After several days everyone was satisfied, and the band settled down for a longer stay near this supply of food. They camped along the east shore of the lake for many days, until the sun was high in the sky and the heat was building up to full summer. Their shelters and garments was ragged, but their bellies was full.

"Again there was a council of the leaders of what was left of the families that made up the band. Again Running Bear spoke out. 'We are filled with fish,' he said. 'We are not starving, but we will get tired of fish. We must have the meat of animals. Most of all, we need their skins for our garments and our shelters. We must leave this place to find bigger animals for meat and skins.'

"The argument went on for three suns. Finally, there was agreement: For six suns they would catch and dry fish while five of their best hunters scouted westward. If they brought back a good report, they would all go on toward the direction of the sunset.

"After five days, the hunters returned excited and happy. In a range of low hills to the west they had found lakes, smaller but deeper, with trees around them for shelter and firewood. Near the lakes were herds of very fast animals only a little smaller than the deer that had given them meat and skins in the East. These animals seemed to have good skins, the hunters reported, and they thought they could catch and kill a few of them. But they had gone beyond the lakes to look down on a plain of deep, waving grass. On that plain they had seen a herd of giant, shaggy animals, each with a hide big enough to shelter a small family. They didn't have time to go close, but the animals looked slow, as if they could somehow be caught and killed. They brought back a skull of one of those animals, complete with horns, to show how big it was.

"The news turned the camp into an uproar. 'We are saved,' the women cried. 'There will be good times again, with meat and fish, skins to fashion garments and to make shelters from the cold.'

"The band was anxious to move to the new lakes with the quick animals near them, and near the bigger animals to be scouted and killed. The leaders agreed to pack up and move at the second sun. They crossed the small trickle of a river at its source, leaving behind their first, new lake, giving it the Indian name for Traverse — crossing over. They could always return there for fish, if the new lakes proved to be poor fishin'.

"When they arrived at the place near the top of the range of hills described by the scouts, they was excited by the cool, wooded hills and the small, blue lakes later to be called Pickerel, Enemy Swim and Blue Dog. It was a land something like that from which they had been driven, but better. They felt it was theirs, their new home.

"They was happy when they thought about the giant animals waiting out on the plains to feed them with their meat and keep them warm with their hides.

"There was fish in the small, blue lakes. They would not starve here. There was young trees to use for framing new shelters, and dead trees for firewood. Right away the young hunters was able to corner and kill a few of the speedy antelope to add some variety to their diet.

"The family leaders met and agreed they would

make a permanent camp here. They would settle down in these wooded hills. This was a good place for a real home. They could defend themselves here, stay long, raise young boys into strong hunters and fighters, and marry and mate and raise another generation. From their new home they could post lookouts to watch to the east, across the valley of The River That Runs North, for enemies that might be followin' or searchin' for them.

"From here they could hunt westward on the great plain that rolled out as far as the eye could see, hunt for the great animals their scouts again came back to tell them about. They unpacked their poor bundles of possessions, clothing and utensils. The older men an' women began to put together poles and willow branches to build a strong, safe village.

"The stronger men, after a few good meals of fish, an' a few days to rest an' repair their killin' weapons, prepared for a big hunt to try to bring a supply of meat back to the new home of the band.

"Twenty-three hunters went out on that first hunt to the plains of Dakota. They moved careful, steady, with scouts ahead an' to the sides, watchin', searchin' the draws and creek beds for animals an' for danger, scannin' the horizons for the big animals they had seen.

"On the second day, just after the sun had reached the top of the sky, they found them in a tall-grass meadow near a small, swampy lake. They was giant, ugly beasts, with huge heads an' bulging shoulders that tapered to small, sleek rear ends. They had big, curved horns and ragged, shaggy manes that seemed to cover their entire front quarters."

"Gosh, I sure would have been scared," Freddie broke in. "Wasn't they afraid of gettin' killed?"

"Well, they couldn't afford to be too scared," John Bear said. "They had to have meat and skins. That was

THE HUNTERS

their life. That was the job of these hunters. Sometimes they got killed doin' it."

He continued. "It was a small herd, about thirty bulls, cows an' calves, standin' knee-deep in the mud at the edge of the swamp, bunched close to protect each other from the flies, tails switching, calves bawlin'. They had fed all morning, were full of grass an' sleepy. They wasn't aware of the hunters that had appeared slowly from behind a rise in the ground, and dropped out of sight.

"The hunters gathered quickly behind a small hill for a meetin'.

"'Big, very big, with thick skin an' bad horns,' one whispered.

"'We can kill them,' another said softly. 'We must all attack one animal.'

"It was agreed they would try to separate one cow in the swamp. One group would attack the head to try to put out the eyes and damage the skull. Another gang would attack her mid-section with spears to try to puncture her lungs, maybe even a lucky thrust to the heart. The most daring hunters would attack her legs with axes, to try to cut her ham strings and tendons, and bring her down so they could finish her off with spears and knives.

"It was two hundred yards from the hiding hill to the buffalo. The hunters began to crawl slow and careful, mostly under cover in the tall grass. The animals didn't see them. At one hundred yards, they could be seen, and some heads came up in the herd. But the animals stood fast. They were curious about these new creatures moving slowly toward them on their prairie.

"The hunters figured that the buffalo was alert and curious, but not afraid. At about fifty yards, the hunters stood upright. The herd turned to watch them, but stood its ground. Several of the bulls moved to the front, lowered and tossed their heads, emitting short, deep bellers. Slow an' quiet the hunters moved toward the nervous animals. At twenty yards, the herd began to move about nervous. Running Bear slowly raised his spear to point to a medium-sized cow near the middle of the herd.

" 'That one,' he said. 'Run!'

"All twenty-three hunters closed in on the cow as the bulls give way and the herd scattered, snorting and bawling. She tried to follow the others, but was surrounded by grunting, gasping hunters, thrusting, sticking, hacking, and then she was down. A long, bone knife was thrust into her throat. As the blood flowed, her wild eyes glazed over and the thrashing of neck and legs stopped. She was dead.

"With the bone knives and the axes, they began to cut her open as she lay on her side. Her intestines poured out, hot and steaming. The big liver was pulled free and chopped into pieces. Each hunter tore into his hot, bloody, raw piece, gnawin' and chewin' the tender meat. The heart also was taken out, still twitchin', an' chopped into pieces. The hunters divided it and chewed it down.

"Filled up with fresh meat, five of the hunters were left to skin and butcher the beast, dividin' the bloody chunks of meat into piles on the hide spread out on the coarse swamp grass.

"The others set out to try to kill another cow. The herd had galloped away about a half-mile, and were now clustered facin' the hunters comin' from the fallen cow. The buffalo were not yet afraid of these strange, two-legged things, but were watchin' them careful. A few of the younger animals and cows had started to graze again, trustin' the big bulls to protect 'em.

THE HUNTERS

"The hunters figured the plan careful. No longer did they have surprise to let 'em to get close. They decided to surround the herd and again attack one animal. When they was close to the herd, Running Bear again pointed to the animal to be surrounded and hacked down. Because the herd was still gentle, it worked again. With more trouble this time, and with some bruises to the hunters, they again brought an animal down and killed her.

"By the time they opened her up and took out the liver and heart it was almost dark. They decided to camp in the open by the second carcass. They began to haul the pieces from the first kill to the new carcass, to collect and protect all the meat. Scooping drinking water from the swamp with their hands, they wrapped themselves in the few ragged clothes each had, and slept through the cool, late-summer prairie night.

"As the sun come up over the low hills, the hunters set about hackin' up the second animal, gathering the wet, slippery meat into piles for each man to carry. Two would stagger back home to camp under the weight of the shaggy, dripping hides, the rest would carry the meat.

"Before noon, they was ready to start back to their new home, each carrying a heap of wet, red meat, tied into a bundle with bits of hide, intestines and reeds from the water hole, and carried as comfortable as possible on back, shoulders or head. The loads was heavy, nearly seventy pounds. After a few miles under the late summer sun, they was sweatin' an' had to stop to rest near a small stream.

"Carrying and sometimes resting, they wearily dragged on up the low hills toward the camp. By nightfall they was exhausted, but happy. After a meal of raw meat and water, they slept again under some willows by a small stream. At the end of the second day they straggled into camp, to be greeted with a great hullabaloo by them who had stayed behind.

"There was a fire already burnin' in camp. The women took charge, cuttin' the meat into smaller pieces, makin' willow spits to toast it over the fire. At first it was eaten barely warmed, mostly raw. The cookin' and feastin' went on all night. By dawn most of the people was asleep, filled up with the red meat and cracklin' fat of the buffalo. A few of the women moved about the camp, gatherin' up pieces of meat, placin' them in hides or pots, and startin' the preparation and tanning process of the two giant hides that had been dragged back to the camp.

"The camp woke in the afternoon heat and again gorged on the meat that was gettin' a little ripe by now, eatin' more slow and less wasteful this time, and afterward an evenin' of carousin' an' dancin', an' a good night's sleep.

"After the second day's feast, they cut the remaining meat into thin strips an' laid it out on a grid of willow branches to dry, keepin' it for future eatin'.

"On the third day, a group slowly gathered to decide what to do. They was happy with their growin' camp on the high ground, next to the cool, fish-filled lakes. But their main source of food was thirty miles or more to the southwest, on a flat, treeless prairie, slopin' downward to the west, toward the rivers they had not yet seen.

"In this band each family, each lodge, had an equal vote. Who was boss was not clear-cut. Leadership come up for each situation, dependin' on the wisdom of the man's thoughts on the problem, and upon the forcefulness of his talk. The people palavered with few words, but with a strong force of their ideas, put out by wavin'

THE HUNTERS

their hands, by the sound of their voices and the fire in their eyes. The problem solving was slow, with much thinking, long pauses and smoking. It was a sure, fair way to decide in the shade of the trees by the lake.

"On the second day, agreement come out for a plan, and then the parts of the plan. They would break into two camps. Most of the women an' older men, an' three of the strongest, fastest young men would remain in the high lake camp. The hunters and twelve women would set up a huntin' camp out on the flat grassland. The women would keep the huntin' camp in order, do the cookin' and with whatever time they had left, would help with the skinnin' and cuttin' of the meat.

"One of the young men at the base camp would always be far to the east, watchin' for enemies that might still be chasin' them from the land of their birth. If such danger showed up, one of the three would be a runner to the huntin' camp, for help. The rest, including the elders and the women, would fight a rear-guard retreat until they joined with the people from the huntin' camp to make a stand and defend their territory.

"It was agreed that this would be their home. No longer would they retreat. If attacked they would die, if necessary, to hold this land. They meant to hang on and grow here at the edge of the plains. If the hunt was good, there would soon be a pack trail of carriers hauling the meat and hides from the hunting camp up the long slope to the permanent camp in the hills.

"Early in the fall, just as the birds was beginning to flock together for their long flight south, an' the late-summer prairie flowers was beginning to fade, the hunters set out to where they hoped to find the buffalo herd.

"The great gods of the earth and sun were kind to the tribe that autumn. They found several herds, and the hunt was successful. They killed eleven buffalo with their spears, axes and knives. Several hunters were injured, but only one was killed by the thrusting, slashing horns and the plungin' hooves. The cuttin', curin' and haulin' of meat and skins went on as the leaves turned to gold and brown and fell from the trees, an' the prairie winds turned cool and the nights frosty.

"They was tired and sore, but happy. The families would be warm an' well fed that winter. They would huddle close together in their new buffalo-hide tents, eat when they was hungry, an' gain strength for their life in the new land.

"Boy, it sounds like they had it pretty good," I said.

"They did for a while," John Bear replied. "For several generations they got along real good. An' I told you how the horses changed their lives. But after the white settlers came, the buffalo disappeared from this part of the country an' the goin' got pretty rough. You know the rest," he said

John Bear got slowly to his feet and started toward the road. After a few steps he turned and gave us the old, palm-out salute. "So long, kids." he said

"G' bye Mr. Bear. Thanks for the story. Come again," we chorused. He grinned and walked on home.

Dust

In the fall of 1932, my parents and all the families of the community were worried about the drought. There had been a severe shortage of moisture for the crops and pastures for a couple of years. That summer it had rained hardly at all, only a few showers that barely laid down the dust for a few hours. In the night, I could hear my parents in the next bedroom talking worriedly about the stark problems of foreclosure and survival.

The grain crops had burned brown and dried up. Most fields weren't even harvested. The grass on the grazing ranges had dried up and disappeared, to be replaced by the coarse, drought-resistant tumbleweeds.

In early fall, with still no rain, the wind picked up and the great dust storms began to roll in from the northwest. I tried my best to help Dad and Mister Brown scratch together enough feed to keep the livestock alive over the winter. I watched the prairie change.

The top soil sifted and rolled, particle grinding against particle as it retreated before the wind, pulverizing itself into ever finer texture, until the slightest breeze would lift it and carry it along in dark, frightening clouds. Drifts of deathly dry, fine powder were building up wherever there was a solid obstacle to stop and hold it. Any baffle to break the straight line of the interminable wind would build its growing drift of rich dust, then move on to form another dune somewhere down the wind.

On an afternoon in November, the wind was thundering and howling around the tiny one-room country schoolhouse. We could hear an occasional "thwump" when a giant, rolling tumbleweed slammed into the side of the building, slowly scratching along the side, then breaking away and resuming its roll until a fence or other obstacle stopped it permanently to help form one of the giant ridges of weeds and dust.

The morning had been dry and cold, with a modest breeze from the northwest. There was some dust, but visibility though cloudy and hazy, was pretty clear for nearly a mile. The sun was a dull, red ball, slowly rising from behind the eastern hills. The sky was a yellowish gray, changing color and density as the high, hazy waves of dust moved over.

When we woke that morning, the bedding and floors were gritty with dust, but we were used to it. We knew that Mother would shake out the dust and sweep the house thoroughly. By the time we returned home from school, the house would smell dusty, but it would be clean.

We walked past the cattle yards as we headed off to school. Mister Brown gave us a wave from where he was pitching some poor-quality hay into the cattle feeding yard.

"You kids be careful today," he called. "I got a feelin' we're goin' to see some wind and dust before dark."

The long walk to school was cold, but uneventful. We buckled down to our class work.

At noon the wind began to rise and visibility outside the schoolhouse windows began to shorten up. At lunchtime we could still see the Georgens' place; by three o'clock, it had disappeared in the waves of billowing dust. Dust storms didn't frighten us any more. We knew that eventually, by six o'clock, or by dark, or by midnight, or by tomorrow, the wind would die down, the dust would settle, and we would be able to see again.

It was Election Day, and in our township the voting was done in Knickrehm's garage. There had been some cars moving slowly past the school since noon, crawling along the fading, lightly graveled road toward Knickrehm's farm. I had begged to go along to see the voting. I convinced by parents and Miss Bjerke it would be good for my learning. I waited by the road until they picked me up.

When my parents, me, and my little sister, Helen, entered the polling place, there were twenty or more people there, restlessly moving about, looking worried and talking, talking.

Clair Cowan edged over to where my Dad was greeting another neighbor. "We've got to vote this Roosevelt in, Frank. We've got to have some help, or we're not going to make it . ." he said.

Clair was a young, scarecrow-thin man of medium height. His face was furrowed with deep vertical lines, dirt lodged in the wrinkles. He hadn't shaved for several days (very few of the farmers shaved more than once a week). The dusty stubble of his beard added to his unkempt, scruffy appearance. On top was a thin thatch of wild hair. He wore a wrinkled, dark gray, ragged shirt, medium-clean bib overalls, and a tattered, blanket-lined denim jacket. He was rugged, haggard, and a little dirty, not entirely out of keeping with the group of worried ranchers and farmers.

"I'm broke, Frank," he continued. "I'm finished

Our family on the prairie

if I don't get some help. All I've got left is a few cows and pigs, and some chickens. I can't keep my animals alive. They've got just about nothing to eat, Frank."

My Dad shook his head and kicked at some rope on the floor of the garage.

"We can't get ourselves out of it, Frank. We don't have anything. We are broke, busted, buried under the dust and thistles. My kids are starting to go hungry, Frank. We don't have enough to eat. We can't get ourselves out of this mess. We've got to have help.

"Jesus, Frank, I don't know what to do. I don't know what to do." Tears rose in Clair's eyes. He turned toward the wall to hide his face. Then he ran his hand over his eyes. "I don't know what to do, Frank. I'm ashamed."

My Dad looked at the floor and shook his head, and turned away. Then he turned back and awkwardly put his hand on Clair's shoulder, then took it away. "Don't give up, Clair. You're not alone. We've got to look out for each other. We'll help each other."

It was a long speech for my Dad.

Others in the garage had heard the conversation and looked away.

"We've got to stick together." It was Ivy Sanders, Freddie's mom, speaking softly, almost as if to herself. "If we stick together and maybe get a little help, we'll stay alive."

"This fella, Roosevelt, sounds like he is goin' to try to help us," someone ventured.

Ivy spoke up again. "I ain't so sure. How can he know what kind of a dust bin hell we got out here. He don't have any idea what it would take to help us pull through this thing. Look out there. Nothing but raw dust, thistles and wind. The animals is dying. We're all dying. How could some guy from New York in fancy clothes, sittin' in a big mansion, have any idea what to do about this God-awful mess?"

She paused. Nobody took up the challenge.

"But, whatever he does, it might be better than what we got now," she continued. "Now we don't have nothing. We're darn near finished."

"Well, he's not elected yet. We'll have to wait until tomorrow to find out. Maybe he can help us, maybe he can't. A lot of other people need help, too, I suppose." It was Rose Knickrehm, Fred's wife.

"Yeah, we got to try to help ourselves, we've got to try to stick it out awhile," Clair Cowan said, his courage back but looking a little sheepish.

"I think the County's got a little relief money left," Fred Knickrehm said. "Maybe we can get a little help, a few dollars for those that have to have it to keep going.

"In the meantime, we've got to finish this voting and take the ballot box to the County, if we can get there in this storm. Has everybody voted?" Heads nodded, and Fred went to the door to see if anybody else was coming up the driveway.

"I'll hold the voting open until five o'clock," Fred decided.

"It's almost four o'clock, Lydia. We'd better pick up Mary at the school and head for home," my Dad said.

When we went outdoors, we were surprised to see that it appeared to be dark, like dusk, even though it was only late afternoon. We could barely see the road, less than a hundred feet away at the end of Knickrehm's driveway. The flying dust, punctuated with shreds of weeds and an occasional tumbling thistle, was flowing from the northwest to southeast on a near-horizontal plane.

Dad started up the old Chevrolet and crawled out onto the road. We could tell we were on the road by the crunch of the gravel beneath the wheels. Dad had his face thrust forward almost to the windshield, staring past the left front fender, watching for the road. The dust came in waves and rushes. It rolled like a storm on Big Stone Lake. Between waves, I could get a glimpse of the road.

I strained over the back seat to look out the windshield as we crawled along, sweating out the mile to the schoolhouse. We finally crossed the narrow iron bridge over Dry Run, then passed the driveway going to the Benson's farm. The schoolhouse should be next, about three hundred yards on the left. Through the gloom and hurtling dust and weeds, we eventually could make out the shadow of the tiny building, standing all alone in the storm.

Dad found the driveway and turned into the schoolyard, easing around the building to place the car on the lee side, sheltered from the wind, driving dirt and debris. My parents sat back in the front seat, slumped in relief.

"Great goodness, do you think we can make it home, Frank?" Mother asked.

"It might let up a little as the sun goes down, sometimes does. We sure don't want to spend the night in the schoolhouse."

"What about the other children? How will they get home?"

"Let's go inside and see what's going on."

The other children were standing in the doorway as we walked around the corner and stepped up on the porch.

My sister Mary ran to Mother and clasped her hand with both of hers. The other children crowded around, trying to ignore the great, black storm outside. Miss Bjerke stood behind them all, smiling and trying not to appear too concerned. She was twenty-two years old — one year out of "Teacher's College" and two year's teaching experience in another country school such as this one. She was sturdily dressed in a wool skirt and woolen plaid shirt.

"Everybody all right, Min?" Dad greeted her warmly.

"We're OK," she said. "Mr. Benson came over about an hour ago and said he would come and get us if it got really bad, so I guess he will be here soon. Come on in out of the wind."

We children milled around the three adults, looking from face to face and then again out the window at the roaring dust storm. The adults made small talk about the election, the schoolwork, the storm, stalling while they decided what to do. As they talked, Leslie Benson's bulky shaped loomed up in the driveway. He lumbered into the yard and through the open schoolhouse door.

"Whew, that's a rough one," he exclaimed. "I started across the pasture, then decided to cut over and follow the fence line so I wouldn't get lost in my own front yard. Mother Nature chose election day to put on the worst dust storm I've ever seen."

"Listen, Frank," he continued, "don't try to get home. You and your family walk over to our house along the fence line, together with Miss Bjerke, my kids and the rest of the kids. We'll just stay there until this thing lets up a little. Then you can come back here and drive your car home. That goes for you two Day kids, too. You just come over to our house until the storm dies down."

My Dad thought about it for a minute, while we watched. We were hoping he'd agree with Mr. Benson, so we would all go over there to a party atmosphere until the storm abated.

"No," Dad said slowly. "Thank you very much for the invitation. Thanks just the same, but I think we'll try to make it home from here. Got the livestock to look after, and the house. It's better we work our way home."

"OK, Frank. You folks sure are welcome to come on over. Belva would enjoy the company. Pretty gloomy over at our place, too, you know. But you know what you have to do. I'll take Miss Bjerke and the rest of the kids home with me."

Mary and I were downcast. "Gosh, Dad, don't you think we ought to stay with the others? It looks pretty bad out there." I hated to be left out of the after-school adventure with the other children.

Mary tugged at Mother's sleeve. "Let's stay,

Mom. It's kinda scary to go home now."

Johnny Bear was looking worried. "We've got our horse, Mr. Benson. Can we bring him along?"

"Gosh, yes! I forgot about your horse. We'll just put him in our barn. We'll leave a note on the schoolhouse door if anybody comes lookin' for their kids. I think everybody would know they are safe at our place."

We were ready to go. "Thanks, again, Leslie. We really appreciate your looking after the children and the school like you do."

"Aw, golly, Frank, I think of them all as my own kids," he chuckled. "Listen, you turn around and come back to our place if it gets too tough. We'll be glad to have you."

"We'll give it a try. C'mon children," Dad said.

Mother bundled Mary into her coat, scarf and wool cap, while the rest of us wrapped our garments tightly about ourselves, with special care to wrap well around the throat to keep out the dust. We worked our way around the corner to the car. The three of us kids crawled into the back seat, with Helen snuggled between Mary and me to keep warm. Dad started the car and eased it around the schoolhouse to the driveway and back out to the road.

As we started almost blindly down the bumpy road, there suddenly was a lull in the roaring dust storm. We could see for nearly a hundred yards. We were driving beside a pasture, virgin sod, and its soil wasn't blowing. The native grass clung to the earth with a root system that had been developing for centuries, through drought, winter freezes and summer rains. It held the earth from blowing away. It wasn't green, but it wasn't moving; it wasn't retreating horizontally before the wind as was the tilled soil.

We moved steadily along the road for nearly half

a mile, then the blowing dust swept into us again. The Georgens' place loomed up on the left. We could see a kerosene lamp in the window on the downwind, protected side of the house near the road. It was only late afternoon. Clarence Georgens stepped out of the rickety door of the barn and waved. We children waved back, although it was doubtful that he could see us. Clarence was a good person, friendly and generous, but not a great farmer.

Dad and Mother were too busy staring past the fenders trying to see the road to look up and wave. At the Georgens' place, a grove of dying willows protected the road from the blinding storm for a short way, then the visibility closed down again. Dad couldn't see past the hood of the car.

"We've got to stop, Lydia. I can't see a thing, can you?"

"No, no. I can't either. I've never seen it this bad."

They sat there for several minutes with the motor running, waiting for the dust to ease up enough to get a glimpse of the road. There was no let-up in the choking blinding, blur.

Mary, who was old enough to recognize danger began to whimper. "Mama, I'm scared. What if the car blows over? Are we going to suffocate?"

Helen was still snuggled low between us, but her eyes were round and frightened. I was trying not to be afraid.

"Don't be such a scaredy cat," I said to Mary. "Dad will get us home somehow."

Mom and Dad looked at each other and Dad smiled a tight, grim, smile. "He's right. I'm going to get out and walk in front of the car, with my right hand on the left front fender. I will be able to feel the road with my feet. Lydia, you put the car in low gear and just crawl along beside me. Howard, you get in front and help her watch for me and the road. We'll get home."

"All right, I'll try it," Mother said. "My goodness, Frank, I never thought it would come to this."

Our system of inching along with Dad walking and occasionally tapping on the fender was working. It took us nearly an hour to cover the remaining mile and a half to our farm. Several times we stopped to rest from the tension for a few minutes. A couple of times Dad became sufficiently disoriented to wander off the road into the shallow ditch. He led the car into a position of dangerously tipping, or so it seemed to the passengers blindly following him. But the panic passed, the gasps and cries from Mary and Mother relieved the tension, and we got back on the road upright and continued.

A dim, peaked rectangle began to emerge on the right side of the road, taking form, then disappearing in the next surge of wind, dust and debris. Soon the tiny house took full form, with a faint light in the south-facing window. Dad walked the car up the short driveway and around the corner of the house to the sheltered side by the kitchen door. Mother turned off the engine, and everyone relaxed a little and sat back in the strange silence, though they could hear the wind howling over the top of the house. Dad placed both hands on the fender, leaned forward on his arms and shook his head. He grinned at Mother, who was slowly relaxing her two-handed grip on the steering wheel.

She rolled down the window, leaned out, looked at Dad, then at the house. "We're home," she sighed. "Thank God, we're home."

Dad looked at her with a long, slow look, as we children began to grow restless and vocal in the back seat of the car.

Our home after a blizzard

"Some home," he said softly.

Mister Brown came around the corner of the house. "I got the milk cows and them calves in out of the storm. They hadn't gone far, and they was glad to come in," he said.

"Thanks, Brown. You're a good help. I'll get over there and we'll do the milking and feeding. Hope they're not very hungry. We don't have much for them to eat," Dad said.

The next morning the wind was down to a breeze. The air was hazy with unsettled dust. It was cold, but we could see for more than a mile down the road toward the school. Dad took us to school in the car, using precious gas he needed for the tractor.

At noon Leslie Benson stopped at the school to tell Miss Bjerke and us children that Franklin Roosevelt had been elected President. I didn't know exactly why the adults seemed so enthusiastic about Roosevelt. I hoped he could make the dust blow a little less, and maybe bring some rain.

But the wind continued to blow, and the dust storms continued. The cattle wandered the pastures looking for something to eat. The weaker animals became sick, and eventually died. Our beef herd began to diminish.

Winter came on in full force, very cold, but not much snow. The snow that did fall blew into small drifts and ridges, and quickly turned black as it became mixed with the shifting dust. One day Milo Cook, the Chevrolet dealer, came out from town with one of his mechanics. The payments weren't being made on the car, he said. He would have to repossess it. Dad gave him the keys to the car, and walked across to his barns without further word. We had heard that some of the farmers had driven the bankers and machinery dealers from their land with rifles and shotguns that winter. That year, the sheriff wasn't enforcing repossessions. But my Dad wasn't a violent man.

We were without a car. We had several horses capable of pulling a buggy or a sleigh. But we weren't in the mood to travel by horse-drawn conveyances, except on the country roads to school. We were an automobile family and had not traveled "to town" with horses for years. We stayed at home that winter, except for school and necessary shopping for supplies. When we absolutely had to have a car for something, Mick would lend us his ancient Model T Ford.

We children usually walked to school, backs turned to the wind and dust, faces and eyes shielded with mittened hands. We wore layers of coats and clothing handed down from sisters, parents and cousins. Not fashionable, but warm. The schoolhouse, with its glowing, coal-burning stove, was a welcome haven at the end of the bone-chilling journey. We gathered around the stove and learned at a steady, enthusiastic pace. It was an isolated, safe environment, ideal for studying with concentration.

As spring approached, people had agonizing decisions to make. Should they go to the expense of planting the crops? Would it rain enough to get the seeds started, or would they literally blow out of the ground. Would the powdery, drifting soil support a crop even if it received standard rainfall? If they decided to plant, where would they get the money to buy gas for the tractors, and treatment for the seeds so diseases wouldn't kill the tiny plants before they grew enough to develop a certain inherent toughness to survive?

Fortunately, my Dad had saved a small bin of grain for seed from the tiny crop of the year before.

Then word came to the chilly prairie that there would be some help for those who had no seed, and no money for gas and machinery repairs. The New Deal programs in Washington were beginning to have some effect at this remote outpost of the nation. Along with the NRA (National Recovery Act), the Bank Holiday, and the CCC (Civilian Conservation Corps), there was the AAA — the Agricultural Adjustment Act. Its help wasn't immediate, but a promise. If the farmers and ranchers would follow certain guidelines for conserving the soil, and limit their planting to avoid flooding the weak market with grain, the government would pay them certain cash benefits.

That was enough assurance for the tractor fuel and farm machinery dealers. They made a minimum amount of credit available and a limited planting was underway.

On a Monday morning in March, the car dealer who had repossessed our car drove it into the yard. My Dad was in the yard near the house.

"You should be using this car, Frank. We know

you need it, and we know you will pay for it when you can." He handed the keys to my Dad.

I stood in the yard watching as my Father took the keys and looked at the dealer briefly, saying nothing. Then he turned and strode toward the low, concrete steps at the front door of our house, where Mother stood watching. He handed her the keys.

"Take him back to town," he said.

Day of the Cows

On a summer day in 1934 when I was almost 10 years old, I was up and out of bed as the first orange and gold light began to flow across the ripening prairie, lighting the barns and cattle yards, and the twenty-one cows that were going to be shot that day. I found a clean shirt in the dresser, pulled on some jeans, socks and old tennis shoes. I was excited and ready.

In the kitchen Mother was lighting the wood fire in the range.

"Hi, Mom. Are Dad and Mister Brown up yet?"

"They're doing the chores, and you've got to do yours before you go."

"I'm goin' to do 'em right now, Mom," I said, and left the kitchen and headed for the wood pile.

In less than an hour everybody had returned to the kitchen/dining room for breakfast. I sensed some tension and excitement, but didn't say much.

"We'll drive the cattle two miles straight south to Scheffler's corner, then west to Randolph," my Dad told us. "If we get on the way by seven we should make it there by noon, which is about right."

"Are you sure Howard should go?" Mother asked.

I held my breath while Dad carefully considered.

DAY OF THE COWS

"Yes, I think we need him to drive the team while Brown and I keep the herd going straight. It will get complicated when we pick up other herds along the way."

I released my breath with a long sigh of relief. I had been looking forward to this excitement for weeks.

I had heard snatches of information about the problems with the cattle in discussions between the adults at home and when neighbors stopped to visit. It seemed that because of the depression, not as many people could buy beef. At the same time the terrible drought had reduced our animal feed supply to a pitiful store of shriveled prairie hay, augmented by stacks of thistles, cut green and stacked immediately to try to preserve some nourishment for the winter months.

Also, there had been talk of "brucellosis" and "animal tuberculosis" among the herds, which were catch-all diagnoses for the various illnesses caused by malnutrition, semi-poisonous feed and the pervasive, fine dust of the dying prairie.

The farmer-committeemen of the Agricultural Adjustment Act were called into meeting, and it was decided that the herds would be thinned. The farmers would be compensated for the animals that were destroyed.

Some stockmen fought the program, wanting to keep their herds together as long as they could. Others were glad to turn most of their animals into cash. Compromises were made. The farmers who didn't want the killing had to send a small number to be shot. Those who were most desperate for cash were allowed to send a larger part of their herds. The committees were pretty fair, our Dad said. Dad agreed to have twenty-one of our animals killed for purposes of disease control.

In our area, the committee also chose the place

for the killing and mass burial of the animals. They picked a spot within a quarter-mile of a tiny, inland town called Randolph.

Randolph had never amounted to much. It had been selected as the site for a depot and grain elevator by the Minneapolis and St. Louis Railroad, when the railroad thought that there should be a town located at every six or eight miles of track. But that was too close together, and many of the towns never developed beyond the first promise.

Randolph was such a place. The grain elevator handled a modest volume of business when times were good. The manager of The Peavey Grain Company, Jim Smith, headed up one of only two families in the neighborhood with a regular income. That family also provided a half-dozen students for Randolph's one-room schoolhouse.

The Hites were the other family in Randolph. They operated the general store, post office and gas pump. The gas pump was seldom used. There was no highway through, past or near Randolph, only country roads of dust and gravel, laid out in square miles, serving the widely spaced farmsteads. The farmers didn't buy fancy "pump" gas for their cars. They used tractor gas, which wasn't as peppy as regular octane gas, but "got you there in plenty of time."

The general store was sparsely stocked. What kept the Hites going, sustained them in their cramped living space above the store, was the Post Office. Mrs. Hite was the Postmistress and Mr. Hite was the country route mailman. Every week-day the regional Post Office would send out the Star Route mail truck to the tiny sub-stations across the countryside. It was usually early in the day, depending on the weather. In blizzards and rainstorms, sometimes the mail didn't get through, but that wasn't often. A mail bag was tossed on the porch of the Randolph country store. Mrs. Hite would quickly sort and organize the mail for the delivery route. Usually, Mr. Hite was on his way to deliver the mail before nine o'clock, and back home before noon.

The pay for the mail work was small, but in Randolph it went a long way. The Smiths with their six kids, and the Hites with two, were the population of Randolph — twelve.

Our cattle drive had seven miles to go to Randolph. That wouldn't be far for a car or a horse, or even a man on foot, but for a herd of weak, nervous cattle that had never been on the trail before, it was going to be a four or five-hour struggle. My Dad wanted to be there by noon because he had to help supervise the assembling of all the herds into one, and then handle the final destruction.

To have a rig that would go as slow as the movement of the cattle, Dad had decided to use a team of work horses hitched to a four-wheeled buggy. I would hold the reins of the gentle team pulling the buggy, while Dad and Mister Brown were outwalkers, holding the herd on the slightly graded roadway.

We proceeded this way for the first two miles, until we reached the intersection where we would turn west. There we were met with two additional small herds, two drivers with one herd and one with the other. Now we were beginning to be a cattle drive, with more than sixty head of livestock jostling and churning, gradually moving west along the road, prodded, pushed and guided by six herdsmen.

Three quarters of a mile further, at the long driveway to Goodman's farmstead, we were joined by another small herd. There were greetings all around by the herd drivers, which now included one farmer's wife who didn't want to be left out of the excitement. Also, we now had two men on horseback. The new animals were sniffed, butted and jostled, then the herd continued on its slow, uneven way west. Periodically, one or two animals would make a break across an open field, and the riders would have to race after them, eventually turning them back into the herd.

I heard Mister Brown call across the road to Dad through an ever-growing, soaring cloud of dust raised by the herd. "We better not let this herd get any bigger, Mister. We'll soon be knocking over mail boxes and tearing out fences. If them critters spooks, we'll have a hell of a mess. They ain't trail broke at all."

Dad raised his arm in reply and nodded.

It was now past nine o'clock, the sun was getting high in its climb, and the day was getting hot. Trailing closely behind the herd, nearly lost in the dust, I was beginning to tire of the cattle drive. I was covered with dust, hot and thirsty. The animals, too, were getting tired. Another hour passed and they had only two miles to go. We could see the dust clouds rising in the hot June sky from other herds moving toward Randolph.

Finally, at near-noon, the lead cattle rounded a fence line, and headed diagonally across an open field to the place where an awful trench scarred the earth.

The county highway department had provided a bulldozer and operator, and for several days under the supervision of the committee, it had been gouging a giant trench in the earth, straight up on both sides and one end. The other end was a gradual slope from the ground level to the bottom of the pit. It would be the grave for all those cattle.

Soon there began to assemble a moving, bawling mass of animals, roughly positioned near the top of the gradual incline leading to the bottom of the trench.

DAY OF THE COWS

A dark green car marked U.S. GOVT. turned into the field. The driver got out, dressed in a clean, pressed uniform, in sharp contrast to the ragged and dusty farmers. He visited briefly with the farmers near him, then strolled over to where my Dad and other Committee members were beginning to assemble.

"I'm Frank Dolby. I'm a Department of Agriculture inspector, and I have been assigned to oversee this operation. Just show me how you plan to do this."

Dad took a step forward. "Well, we plan to herd all these cattle into the trench at once, down the ramp at the open end. Then we will close that end with those gates you see piled over there, and drive down some steel posts to hold them in place. We think all the cattle will fit closely into the pit. They will all be standing.

"When we have the gates in place and solidly fastened, everyone will pull back except the four riflemen who will do the shooting. There are one hundred and fifty-three head of cattle in this bunch. I have the official tally here, all on the forms we were given."

"OK," Dolby said. "It looks all right to me. We are supposed to be as humane as possible. I want to be damned sure all those cattle are dead before you start dozing dirt back on them." He looked at the group with the rifles. "OK, guys?"

"Got it," one of them said.

"All right, go ahead with it. I'll stay around until it is finished. And for God's sake be careful with the shooting, and don't forget about ricochets. We sure don't want anybody hurt or killed. And get those kids away from here."

There were only two of us boys in the group of livestock farmers — me and Freddie Sanders. Neither of us wanted to leave just when the real excitement was going to begin. I looked at Dad, and he shook his head.

Just at that time, Mr. Hite from the general store in Randolph walked over. He had hiked across the field to observe the frenetic activity in his backyard.

"Listen, Frank, those boys could come on over to the store. My kids are going to make some ice cream, and the boys could help," he said.

Freddie and I moved closer together. "I don't want to make no ice cream," Freddie said softly into my ear.

"Heck, no," I replied. "I wanta see them shoot those cows in that pit."

"Boys, that's a mighty fine invitation from Mr. Hite. I think you had better take him up on it." Dad had moved over to stand directly in front of us.

"Gee whiz, Dad. I wanted to see them shoot those cows."

"I'm sorry, Howard. It's too dangerous. You heard what the inspector said. Anyway, you like ice cream."

I edged closer to my Dad. "We don't want to go over there and be with those Hite kids," I whispered.

Dad's face became stern. "I want you to go over to Hite's store, Howard. You and Freddie go, right away."

I knew the argument was over. My Dad was usually kindly and lenient. But when his face was stern, we children didn't even consider further argument.

When we got to the store, the ingredients for making ice cream were ready. Alice and Maurice Hite were putting together the mechanical ice cream maker, powered by a hand crank.

"Hi, Freddie — and Howard," Alice greeted us.

Alice was twelve, a year older than Freddie, but she really liked him. They didn't go to the same school, so the difference in their ages wasn't so important. She was always moving close to Freddie at community gatherings and whispering to him. Freddie didn't much care for her, but girls didn't bother him.

Maurice was the same age as Freddie and I. He was slender and pale, with a soft, high voice. He stayed inside a lot, and didn't rough-house and play ball and tag at the summer picnics.

"C'mon, Freddie, let's go around and get the ice." Alice was actually tugging at Freddie's sleeve, excited about going into the dark icehouse with him.

"Ick, that's disgusting," Maurice said to me after they had gone. "She is so boy-crazy it makes me sick. She just makes a fool out of herself."

I said nothing. I didn't want to have a conversation with Maurice. I was angry and embarrassed to be there . I was humiliated to be making ice cream with these children when out there, less than a quarter-mile away, was a violent drama as the riflemen killed the cattle.

Alice and Freddie returned from the ice house with two big chunks of ice in a children's wagon. Freddie was carrying a small hatchet with which they would hack and shave the ice into small pieces to pack around the cylinder inside the wooden bucket of the mechanical ice cream maker.

I didn't take part in that activity. Making ice cream seemed trivial and revolting to me. I sulked and leaned against the porch, not watching. On the other hand, Freddie Sanders was a survivor. If the situation called for making ice cream, he'd make ice cream until the situation changed and he could do something more appropriate for his free spirit. He enthusiastically took charge of the project, with Alice hovering as close to him as possible, and Maurice grudgingly doing most of the work and turning the ice cream maker. The cylinder ground slowly around, embedded in the chopped ice, churning and mixing the cream and sugar concoction inside. Then we heard the first crack! crack! crack! of the high-powered rifles

The activity on the porch stopped. We heard the crack! of the fourth rifle. Then the firing began to take on a steady rhythm — crack! crack-crack! crack!

Freddie came over to where I was standing by the wall looking across the field toward the firing. "They're really dropping 'em now. We oughta see this."

"I thought all you wanted to do was make ice cream and goo goo eyes at that girl," I growled.

Freddie grinned. "Let's get the hell outa here and go see them shoot them cows."

"We're not supposed to go. Both my Dad and the Inspector said we had to stay away."

"Crap!" Freddie spat into the dust at his feet. "We ain't ever goin' to see anythin' like this again. We gotta get over there an' see what it looks like."

"You mean sneak over?"

"Yeah. We can make it over and back by sneaking along the railroad tracks and crawling through them weeds. We can get close enough to see somethin'."

"What about Alice and Maurice? They'll tell on us."

Freddie looked first at Alice, then Maurice, who were watching and listening. The ice cream making was forgotten for the moment. "They won't tell on us." The other two children said nothing, but Freddie was confident his influence over them would hold up.

"OK. Let's go," I said, a little breathlessly. My heart was already beginning to pound. I could feel it bumping against my T-shirt.

We slipped across the yard and the dusty road, then over the graded, weedy railroad track, and worked our way along the ditch beside the track. We could hear the firing of the rifles getting louder and closer.

I started to crawl up the bank to look over at the scene, but Freddie called me back with a harsh whisper. "Come back down here. We ain't far enough yet." He crawled half-way up the bank to where I was clutching the earth. "I think we gotta go as far as that second pole down there to be across from the pit."

"Jeesus!" I whispered. "If we do that we're going to tear our clothes to pieces on the weeds and junk along the track."

"That's OK by me. It's worth it. We gotta see this thing." The shooting sounded nearer now, and we could hear the muffled bawling of the terrified cattle at the bottom of the pit.

We slid back down the grade, into the ditch along the track, and slowly worked our way along it, being very careful not to rustle the tall weeds any more than absolutely necessary to get through. We were beginning to pick up a good load of brambles and stickers from the dry weeds and thistles.

"Ouch! Jeesus!" Freddie cried out as he came down with his knee on a prickly pile of brambles.

"Shut up, Freddie. You want to get us killed?"

Freddie rolled onto his back and pulled spines out of his knee. "They ain't goin' to kill us if they find us. Ain't you ever been whipped before?"

"Not by my Dad, I ain't. An' I sure don't want to try it. If he ever got really mad at me, it would be hell to pay. Let's keep goin' a little ways farther an' then go up and look."

Freddie, in the lead, was going forward now on all fours, keeping as low as he could. I copied his style. We crabbed along like that for nearly a hundred yards, then Freddie stopped.

"That's it," he whispered as I crawled up, breathing hard. "I think we are right opposite the pit. The weeds are kinda short here. We're goin' to hafta stay really low, and very quiet."

I took a deep breath. "Let's go up," I said.

Slowly we inched our way up to the top of the grade, side by side, until our heads were just even with the ends of the railroad ties. We could see between the ties, beneath the rails, but couldn't get enough of a down angle to see what was going on down the bank on the other side.

"We're gonna have to stick our heads up to see," Freddie said.

"Jeez, I don't know. They are sure to see us."

"Lissen, Howard, we didn't come all this way to quit now. We gotta take a look. I'm goin' up."

Freddie crawled upward, with his head down, until his body was parallel with the railroad ties. Then he slowly raised up and looked over the bank.

"God Almighty, I don't hardly believe it," he exclaimed softly. He dropped back prone and rolled his head until he could see me. "It's hell down there. You gotta see it." His eyes were wide, his face white.

Heart pounding, I eased up toward the top until I was lying flat alongside Freddie, then slowly raised myself up and looked over the drop-off to the other side. We were directly behind the four riflemen, and high enough to see into the pit. One of the shooters was reloading, a second one was just standing looking across the pit. The bolt action was open on his rifle. Smoke curled out of both the muzzle and breech as it cooled down. The other two had rifles up, shooting systematically at moving heads. Crack! Crack! Crack! as they would get off nearly simultaneous shots.

The bottom of the pit was a scene from hell. The floor was nearly covered with prone bodies, many of them twitching and kicking, heads thrashing. The cattle still standing were in total panic, plunging and rearing among the dead and dying bodies, hooves striking down on the heads and bellies of the animals on the ground. Because of the panic in the pit, the shooters couldn't get a clean shot at the heads, so they were bringing them down with shoulder shots, or wherever they could hit a bawling, leaping animal.

The inspector was standing near the end of the line of shooters, staring into the pit and slowly shaking his head. There was nothing to do but keep shooting now until all was quiet down there.

The farmers and ranchers were ranged around the near side of the pit, beside and behind the shooters, out of the way of any stray bullets that might ricochet off a horn or a rock in the pit. Some were still watching the mayhem in the pit. Others had had enough, were looking away or talking softly with neighbors. These were people who lived with animals, and while they may not have loved them, they respected them and cared for their needs as best they could. The horrible agony in the pit was sickening, even to the toughest of them.

"God dammit, get it over with," someone said to one of the riflemen, who had stopped for a breather and to let his rifle cool down.

The rifleman gave him a long look. "You wanta to do this, Bob?" he said. He thrust his rifle toward the farmer. "You think I like doing this? I could puke."

Bob raised his hand in a weary salute, shook his head, and turned away. As he did so, he saw us on the railroad tracks, our mouths open, taking in the wild scene. Bob opened his mouth, about to shout at us, then closed it. He looked at us for a long moment, then raised his arm and motioned us back down the slope. We slowly withdrew across the ties and rolled down the slope.

"My God, what a mess," I gasped.

"Let's get out of here before that guy changes his mind and tells somebody," Freddie said. "Move fast, but don't make any noise."

We fled rapidly back along the ditch toward Randolph and the two children making ice cream on the porch of the store.

Alice and Maurice caught sight of us as we climbed over the railroad track and started across the road toward the general store. Alice couldn't hold back. She ran forward, grasped Freddie's sleeve, and walked with him back to the porch, all the while looking into his face.

"What was it like, Freddie? What's going on? Was it awful?"

Freddie pulled his arm free, climbed onto the porch, looked down at the ice cream maker, then leaned against the wall of the house. "It was bad. It was really bad," he said.

He was going to say more, but paused. Then we all noticed something had changed.

"They've stopped shooting," Maurice said.

"I'm glad that's over." I sighed, sat down on the edge of the porch and put my face in my hands.

"The ice cream is ready. Let's take the thing apart and have some!" Alice was trying to break the gloomy mood and tension.

"I guess I ain't hungry," Freddie said, moving off the porch and poking dust with the toe of his shoe.

"Me neither," I said.

The bulldozer started up. We could hear the deep-throated growl of the big diesel engine, and see the black smoke from its exhaust.

"We gotta go," I said, and started to move off toward the activity in the field.

DAY OF THE COWS

Alice took a step toward Freddie, looking desolate. The ice cream party was breaking up. "Freddie, don't you even want to taste it?" she appealed.

"I couldn't eat any. Anyway, I got to go and catch a ride home. Thanks for asking."

"We'll give you a ride in our buggy." I said. "Let's go."

With a wave to the lonely figures on the sagging porch, we walked rapidly toward the men milling around the pit and bulldozer.

Mister Brown was hitching our team to the buggy when we arrived. The sun was beginning to cast long shadows.

"Can Freddie ride home with us, Dad? We go right by Sanders place."

"Sure, of course. His Dad is riding home with us. How was the ice cream?"

"OK," I replied.

"Just OK?"

"Yeah."

Dad looked at me closely for a moment, and apparently decided not to pursue it. The big bulldozer was roaring and snorting, shooting plumes of black diesel smoke skyward as it steadily pushed load after load of dirt into the pit.

The inspector strode over to my Dad. "I think it went OK. I'll stay awhile to make sure the cover-up is good. That area will have to be leveled out again in about a year. Will you look after that?"

"We'll handle it," Dad replied. "Thanks for helping us with this mess."

"Yeah, it's bad. But it's over."

Several cars were leaving the field, throwing up trailing clouds of dust. Some people were walking away, toward the nearer farmsteads.

"Well, let's get on home," Dad said to our group.

Mister Brown climbed up on the buggy seat on the driver's side, and Dad got up beside him. Mr. Sanders, Freddie and I sprawled across the flat buggy bed at the back. The horses had been resting for hours, and started for home at a frisky pace. The grown-ups talked quietly, rehashing the events of the day. Freddie and I stared pensively at the flat prairie as it flowed past; neither of us felt much like talking.

In half an hour we dropped off Freddie and Mr. Sanders at their mailbox, and headed steadily, silently home. I dozed on the bouncing flatbed. It was nearly dark when the now-weary horses turned into our barnyard, ears pointed forward toward water, feed and rest.

I slowly helped Mister Brown unhitch and unharness the horses while Dad began feeding the other animals. As we finished with the horses, Mother came over bringing the milk pails.

"How did it go?" she asked me.

I looked at the ground, then looked away at the horizon. "It was bad," I said slowly. "You better ask Dad about it."

She looked at Mister Brown, who shook his head. She walked away with the milk pails to find my Dad.

Rocky Rogers

John Bear told us the Sioux Indians believed nobody owns the land. It is in the same domain as the sky, the wind and the rain.

Even so, John W. Rogers was granted title to his 160-acre homestead on the 23rd of January, 1890. His certificate was signed by Benjamin Harrison, President of the United States. I have it in my strong box of mementos. Rocky lived on that tiny portion of the Earth for the rest of his life. I would sit on the floor in the kitchen after supper and listen to my parents and their visitors tell Rocky Rogers stories.

Rocky Rogers came into the scene as a dashing, young pioneer who rallied great grain threshing crews, dominated by Rocky's giant steam engine, which traveled to the far reaches of the territory to perform its unique service. That towering, hulking engine became a landmark for Rocky's farm and his hallmark for the rest of his life.

Somehow times turned bad for Rocky, even before the Great Depression and the dust bowl. His empire disintegrated and turned to dust as the neighborhood watched. He was a bonanza man who soared and prospered, then crashed to earth.

Rocky's corner was the pivot on our way to school. We traveled a mile south to his crumbling homestead, then turned west for a mile and a half, passing only the Georgens' place and Cecil Benson's farm before reaching the tiny, one-room building that miraculously stood up to the raging storms of summer and winter. It creaked and groaned, flapped and banged, but protected its children with the hysterical determination of a mother fox defending her young from a predatory pack of dogs.

When I was in the lowest grades, my Dad hitched up two elderly, trusted work horses to a buggy and my older sisters and I lumbered slowly along to school. Mister Rogers, which is what we called him, would almost always come out of his paintless, one-room homestead shack, or stop his work among his horses, to make sure our rig was going all right. He would smile his scarecrow, broken-toothed smile and wave. My sisters would look away, but I always waved back.

"I watch after them kids of yours, Frank. I make sure that rig ain't mixed up, an' it's goin' straight," Rocky told our Dad.

"Thanks, Rogers, I appreciate it. Let me know if you need something," Dad replied.

"You done good by me, Frank. You been a good neighbor. I'll look after them kids if I kin."

Rocky was a big, raw-boned man, remindful of a starving, longhorned steer. He was slightly stooped, always limping a little from some real or imagined injury. He wasn't actually very old, maybe in his late fifties. He looked old because of his unkempt condition, his ragged clothing and his cadaverous physique. He usually had a stubbly beard and a ragged, self-inflicted haircut. His torn jackets and overalls flapped around him as he moved. He had once been a much heavier man. He really did look like a scarecrow to us.

ROCKY ROGERS

His face always had a dark, greasy cast to it, caused by dirt, whiskers and the salve he created and smeared on himself for "protection". He had a big, craggy, hawk face with large, protruding cheekbones. His jaws and mouth were wide and coarse. A number of teeth were missing at random spaces. The rest were brown with stain from tobacco he chewed, and from the alkaline water he drank from his shallow well.

His dogs seemed to have gathered to themselves the worst features of their genetic trips from the dawn of their species to Rocky's farm. It was a ravening, greedy pack of rejects from the surrounding farms and ranches, from passing travelers, or at the end of long treks from some distant agony of birth. They were held there by the primal instincts of protection and survival — shelter from the elements, and the expectation of an occasional meal.

In the 1930's, the dogs and Rocky survived on horsemeat and welfare surplus food — unmarked cans of evil-smelling meats, bags of beans and flour and, periodically, a can of lard. Dad said Rocky knew how to bake bread, but nobody ever saw any.

The shack was heated with a wood or coal-burning range. He seldom had the money or the means to go to town to buy coal. After his small grove of trees disappeared into the stove, his outbuildings and finally his barn melted away — torn apart, broken up and fed into the stove to keep himself and the dogs from freezing. Finally, only a lean-to part of his barn, unpainted, spavined and gaping, was left to poorly shelter the remaining horses.

Ugly hammer-heads they were, resembling both Rocky and his dogs. Some showed a hint of a long-past gentility, but they had all deteriorated into a bunch of wild outlaws, survivors of limited feeding and care.

Even a young, expert horseman would have had a difficult time controlling them. Rocky eventually gave up on them, his land lay idle, his plow, planter and cultivator broken or rusting away. Even the steam engine began to rust away and deteriorate.

When Rocky had tried to farm his land, the horses would be rearing and plunging in the harnesses. Several times the team ran away with a plow or harrow harnessed to them. They would tear through fences and gallop across the prairie until some neighbor stopped them, calmed them down and brought them home.

One time when Rocky had them harnessed to a disc harrow, they bolted. Somehow he fell forward in front of the machine and the blades of the disc ran over him. My Dad, who saw the horses run, found him in the field covered with dirt and blood, his jacket and overalls in shreds. Dad dragged him aboard a wagon and brought him to our house. He tried to get Mother to wash him up and clean the cuts and wounds with a disinfectant. Rogers was filthy and he stunk, and she wouldn't do it. Dad stretched him out on the porch floor, washed him off and disinfected him just as he would a farm animal that had gotten hurt in a fence or another accident. Rocky was groaning and "seemed to have some busted parts," as Mister Brown observed, who stood watching the operation and giving practical advice. Brown and Dad bandaged him and made him reasonably comfortable on the porch. He was conscious, with mumbling and moaning coming from his battered, lacerated face.

Mother made him some bean and bacon soup. As Dad and Mister Brown fed it to him, he was soon sitting up, slurping the soup and smacking his lips, as he always did over good cooking. Later, Dad brought him blankets. He seemed sleepy, and Dad thought a night's rest would help determine whether they should take him thirty miles to the hospital in Aberdeen for professional medical care.

In the morning, Rocky was gone. Like a wounded animal, he had crawled off to his den to recover. Recover, he did. Dad brought him hot meals over the next few days. Pretty soon he was up and limping around his shack and barn, trying to get his team together again. Dad and Mister Brown where pretty sure he had some broken ribs, which must have been extremely painful. None of the deep cuts and rips in his skin became infected. He lived in so much dirt he was immune to infection, Mother declared.

When my two older sisters graduated from the country school and spent the winter in town with Grandma Krueger to go to high school, Mary and I abandoned the horses and buggy and walked to school. That created some problems.

As Rocky became more and more a ward of the charity system, the five horses he kept alive grew wilder and wilder. We had to walk nearly a mile along Rocky's fence. The fence was steadily breaking down even though Rocky periodically spent some time working on it. Every day the starving horses followed the fence line, stretching their necks toward us, pawing the ground and baring their teeth — actions not very natural for formerly domestic horses.

Were they just being friendly? Or were they so desperately hungry and wild that two small children looked like something to trample and tear with their large, menacing teeth? Every day we watched the horses strain against the frail, barbed wire fence, and we whimpered as we made our way along it to the school.

One day Dad walked with us as far as Rocky's shack and strode over to the fence where Rocky stood.

"My children are afraid of your horses, Rogers. Do you think they might hurt them?"

"Hurt them nice little kids? Hell, no, Frank. They wouldn't hurt them kids even if they did get over that fence."

"Well, the children don't have any protection if the horses got through the fence," Dad said doubtfully.

"My God, Frank, I won't let them horses hurt them little kids. I'll be out here to see to it."

And he was. Day after day. He tried to keep the horses near the barn by withholding their water until it was time for the children to walk by, or by feeding them when he had the feed.

Later, when I was in the sixth grade and traveling alone in the fall before I got the pony, I got braver. If I cut across Rocky's pasture, I could save nearly a quarter-mile of walking on the way to school. But if Rocky's horses, hanging around his shack and barn saw me, they would chase me. It was an exciting gamble. I would try to keep a very low profile in the roadside ditches when approaching Rocky's pasture. When I got there I would roll under the fence, stay low and try to sneak across. If the horses saw me and gave chase, I would run like crazy for the nearest fence and roll under, sometimes just avoiding the ragged, unshod hooves. The next year my route to school would change, and I would look back on those heart-pounding morning jousts with Rocky's horses as a scary but exciting part of growing up.

In spite of Rocky's medical miracles and his animal toughness, his command of his situation gradually began to break down. He lived on free groceries provided by the New Deal dole programs of the l930's, and on horsemeat. (One horse met its Maker every fall, and the frozen carcass could be seen near his shack, covered with an old tarp).

At the same time, I was beginning to feel more grown up. I began to talk a little bit with Rocky. Just short conversations — greetings, really. "Hello, Mister Rogers," or "That's some dog you have there." Some of the dogs liked me and would follow me down the road until Rogers called them back.

I asked him about his steam engine one day. By that time it hadn't run for many years. It was becoming a rusting hulk, like an old steel freighter blown up on the beach. It stood a dozen feet tall, and must have been twenty feet long. The gigantic drive wheels seemed taller than the tallest man in the neighborhood; they were at least three feet wide, with great, jagged lugs to grip the ground.

"She used to run pretty good," Rocky said. "She had a lot of power." Then he walked away.

Three days later when I walked by on my way home, Rocky was out by the steam engine, which stood quite near the fence and the road. "Want to see how she worked?" Rocky asked.

I said, "sure," and crawled under the fence.

Rocky wasn't used to talking to children. He shouted and cursed at his horses and dogs, but he was hesitant and awkward with me. In a halting way, he started to show me how the engine worked. He must have been thinking about this conversation in his lonely shack, and rehearsing it with his dogs for an audience. He was shy, but he loved that engine, or the glory days it recalled.

I followed him as he began to point out parts of the machine and how they worked. "Them big valves there, they used to snap open and shut like rifle shots. An' that big flywheel, when she got up to speed, it would just whir and hum and make a pounding sound like

Prairie steam engine.

thunder. She would belch out smoke from her smokestack that would go a hundred feet in the air. Lotsa times there was fire in that smoke when she was really hammering."

He talked for nearly half an hour about that old decaying hulk of a steam engine, as if it was alive and vibrating with power. Then he finally broke off into silence, and just stood there looking at it. His mouth worked slightly, and his face crumpled with a strange look. Finally, I couldn't look at him. I was embarrassed by Rocky's love affair with the old engine.

"She's all I got," he said finally. Then he looked sheepishly at me. "Them was good times, boy."

I looked at the ground and shuffled my feet. I was uneasy with the situation. "Well, I got to go home, Mister Rogers," I said. "Thanks for telling me."

Rocky stood there gazing at the rusting tower of iron until I was a half-mile down the road, then he turned and, limping slightly, trudged back to his shack.

After that day. the friendship between us made some headway, although there was still considerable caution on both sides.

One afternoon, I was on my way home from school when the old man came out of the house and motioned me over. "C'mon into the house," Rocky said. "I got somethin' I want ter show ye."

I was doubtful. I had never been in Rocky's house. I decided to do it. Rocky opened the wire gate for me, then preceded me to the door and opened it. As I stepped inside my mouth dropped open. It was more like an animal's den than a house. The floor was dirt. Maybe there was a plank floor under it, or had been, but it was dirt now.

On the left was an old iron cookstove, a big one, with a couple of blackened kettles on top of it. On the right was a scaly iron bed propped up on bricks and stones so it was approximately level. Spread over the bed were what might have once been blankets and quilts. They were filthy, black and gray, greasy in texture.

Two of the scrawny dogs were on the bed. Another two were slinking alongside Rogers, peering around him and between his legs, alarmed at a stranger in their den even though they knew me. Low, rumbling growls came from deep in their chests.

Straight ahead, across from the door, was a square, wooden table, scarred and splintered, black with dirt and grease. There was one straight-backed kitchen chair by the table, and not another one in the shack. Beside the table, against the back wall, was an old steamer trunk, bound with oak slats along the top and sides, with leather straps, rotten and torn, belted around it the other way.

"I want to give yer somethin', boy," Rocky rasped.

I just stood there, three steps inside the door, ready to run, gasping at the powerful smell of the room. It was a mixture of coal and wood smoke leaking from the old cookstove, of greasy cooking, and dirt and animal smell emanating from Rocky and the dogs. It wasn't quite overpowering because of the flow of outside air through the chinks in the walls and around the windows.

The atmosphere inside was gloomy, nearly dark. The air was filled with dust motes, kicked up by the animals scurrying around at the approach of the stranger, the tiny particles tumbling and swirling in the weak sunlight beaming through the filthy window.

Rocky went to the back wall to the old banded steamer trunk, kicking and cuffing the dogs out of his way. He fumbled with the straps and latches, and soon had the lid up. A look inside made me quickly draw my breath. Inside it was pristine clean. The inner lining of the trunk and the folded pieces inside seemed to glow in contrast to the dirt and gloom of the hovel. I caught a glimpse of a lace collar, some clean, fine pieces of clothing, photographs and books. Rocky dug down and removed from the trunk a bright, clean, red, white and black woolen blanket. He folded it over his arm, patted it and brought it over to me.

"I got this here in Canady a long time ago," he said. "Got it from the Hudson Bay Company. I was young and workin' for a contractor, hauling dirt with a big, four-horse team. I had some money in them days." He paused, looking away at the floor, thinking back.

"I seen you walk by many times, boy, when it was cold. I seen how cold you was. This here blanket will keep you warm, boy. She is the biggest, best damn blanket I ever seen."

"Are you giving it to me, Mister Rogers?" I asked,

looking up at the lined, coarse face.

"Yep, boy, she's yours."

I hesitated. "I don't know whether I should take it. Maybe I shouldn't."

Rogers was silent for a moment, looking at the blanket, then at me. "Why wouldn't ye take it?"

"Well, I don't know. Maybe you need it more than I do. Maybe I should ask my Dad."

"I want yer to have it, boy. You take it with you. You ask your Dad. Your Dad, he ain't goin' ter make yer give it back. He's a good man, yer Dad."

"I really thank you, Mister Rogers. I sure thank you. I don't know what to say. It's really a great blanket," I babbled.

Rogers stood by his doorway and watched me as I trudged the long mile home. I was puzzled. "I wonder why he did that," I kept asking myself. "He hardly ever talked to me during all those years I've been going by his place. Just that one time about his old steam engine."

Later, when I talked to Mother and Dad about it, they didn't seem so puzzled. They thought the blanket was of a very fine quality, and congratulated me on receiving it.

"Maybe you are the best friend he has," Mother said. "A friend should keep a present from a friend."

"Gosh, I only talked to him a few times," I said.

"Even so, Howard, even so, you were his friend, and he knew it," Mother said.

Rocky Rogers died a few years later, during the first winter I was away at high school. He must have gotten sick, too sick to go for help. He died and froze, and his starving dogs ate some parts of him before Clarence Georgens noticed something was wrong about the place, stopped in and found him.

Beauty

When I started the fifth grade, my older sisters had gone to live with Grandma Krueger in town to go to high school. Helen, my little sister, hadn't started school yet, so I walked the two-and-a-half miles to the one-room country school alone.

As the weather grew colder that fall, Dad became worried about me tramping off alone across the prairie pastures and plowed fields to school. It was a cold and lonely trip.

"I'm going to get Howard a horse to ride to school," he told us one night at supper. "It will be company for you, boy, and it will keep you warm. The Sombkes have that red pony they never ride. I'll bet they'll sell it, or trade for it."

Dad took Ed Sombke aside the next Sunday at church and asked him about it. Mr. Sombke wanted to think about it. The following Sunday they talked again and agreed on a trade — the red pony for a corn shelling machine we didn't use much any more. The next Saturday, in mid-November, Dad and I hitched a team of horses to the old "democrat" buggy, loaded on the corn sheller, and drove the four miles to the Sombke place. We warmed up in their kitchen, then put a leather halter on the horse. Dad would lead him from the buggy seat, while I drove the horses.

Mr. Sombke said the pony hadn't been ridden in the past year, but that the children played with him and he was gentle. Dad and I petted and stroked him, then started slowly, gently toward home. In a little more than an hour we were in our barnyard. I stroked him some more, then turned him loose in a small yard by the horse barn to look about, eat some hay and get acquainted.

The horse was smaller than a quarter horse. Mister Brown suggested that it might be a crossbreed that came from the herd on the Indian reservation, with some mustang blood in it. It had a thick, red coat, with just an etching of black on the mane and tail. Everyone agreed that its name should be Beauty.

On Sunday I tied a short rope to Beauty's halter and led him to the water tank for a drink. He was a little skitterish now, and frisky, but he went along all right, and I got him watered and back to his stall in the barn. I held his halter with one hand and with the other, gently curried the animal's back and flanks. The horse seemed to like the attention, stopped fidgeting, and stood quietly.

In the evening I watered and fed him, curried him some more, and talked to him. Although I was tall for my age, Beauty was too big for me to get aboard without something to stand on — a box, a chair or a low wagon. We hadn't even considered a saddle. After all, part of the reason for the horse was to keep me warm with his body.

Monday morning when it was time to start for school, it was cold and windy and the patches of water around the barns had frozen solid. Dad had watered and fed Beauty when he was doing the early barnyard chores while I was waking up, getting dressed and having breakfast.

When I came over to the barnyard with my lunch pail slung around my neck and under my arm on a piece of light rope, both Dad and Mister Brown were there to see me off. The pony was bridled. He appeared frisky from the good food and confinement of the past day, and a little spooky because of the new surroundings and the three strange people around him.

Mister Brown flipped the reins crisscross over the pony's neck and held his bridle, while Dad put my raised foot in his cupped hand and hoisted me on the pony's back. Beauty's head came up sharply. He jumped and trembled a bit, and at this point I had the feeling this wasn't going to be an uneventful start. I grabbed the horse's mane, not showing the confidence and control that assures an animal.

"Aw, he's jest a little frisky this mornin'. He'll settle down when you've rode him a little way," Brown said.

Both the adults were used to animals, commanding them and dominating them. The possibility of serious trouble from this small horse didn't occur to them. To them the horse seemed small, but to me aboard the trembling horse, he seemed big and dangerous.

Mister Brown let go of the bridle and Dad gave the pony a light slap on the rump, as he would to his work horses when he turned them loose to roll in the dust and grass. The pony reacted differently. He took off with a big jump, with me sliding far back and then to the side. On his third jump the pony landed on one of the icy spots and went sprawling on its side. I was thrown clear and landed on my side on the frozen ground.

The pony thrashed its way to its feet and galloped to a far corner of the barnyard. I lay there slightly stunned. Dad and Brown froze for a second or two, then quickly ran over and knelt by me.

"You hurt, son? Anything broken?" Dad was concerned, but was pretty sure I couldn't have been hurt badly.

I stood up, wobbly, trying not to cry. I was stunned and frightened

"I guess I'm OK. My side hurts. I fell on my lunch box.

"I don't think it is much, son. You seem all right to me." He was sorry about the accident, also a little amused now that it was apparent that I wasn't seriously hurt.

"The best thing, son, after something like that happens is to get right back on and ride him. That way you show him you aren't afraid of him."

Brown had cornered the pony, quickly grabbed one of the reins, and had him in tow. "I think you should get right back on him, boy," Brown said.

I looked at my father. "I don't want to, Dad. Maybe he will fall again."

"The chance that he'll do that again is pretty slim, Howard. That's a gentle horse. He isn't mean. He just needs to be ridden a little."

"Tell you what I'll do," Mister Brown said. "I'll lead 'im a ways until you and that there horse gets used to each other. Then it will be OK."

Dad nodded his approval of the plan. "That's a good idea. Come on, Howard, let's try it again. Mister Brown will lead the horse until he settles down."

"I don't want to ride him, Dad."

He turned stern. "This is something you have to do. Now come here and let's get you up on him."

I came reluctantly forward. With Brown holding the bridle again, Dad hoisted me up on the horse. Beauty was spooky and jumpy, but Brown had a solid, authoritative grip on both reins just under Beauty's jaw.

We started off diagonally across the section toward the school, with Brown firmly holding the bridle and talking soothingly to the horse. "You just stay calm there, horse. Ain't anything to get riled up about. You take that boy to school now," he crooned.

I held the crossed reins with one hand and gripped the horse's mane with the other. I was frightened, uncomfortable and miserable. I hated and feared the horse.

"Boy, you dassen't let the horse know you are scared. Animals, they know them things, they can feel it. This here's a nice pony. You just has to take control of him. You got to let him know who's boss, even if you have to hit him a little. Animals, they need that kinda treatment. Then they knows how to act."

I hung on and said nothing.

After we had gone about a quarter of a mile, Brown stopped. "I think you two has got to know each other now. He should go good now. Don't hold them reins too tight. Give him a little head room, let him run a little if he wants to."

The horse started up again, with me gripping the reins hard with one hand, and Beauty's mane with the other. Both the horse and I were nervous and uncomfortable.

A little more than a half-mile from our place was a line fence used in the summer to divide the big pasture so half could be grazed while the other half was resting or being cultivated or seeded. On Sunday, Brown had walked out and lowered the three strands of barbed wire at the place where the horse and I had to cross on the route to the school. He stapled the wires to the lower end of the fence posts, leaving a space between two fence posts for the horse to cross. The wires were there, still stretched between the posts, about an inch above the ground.

When Beauty and I reached the point where the barbed wire stretched along the ground, the horse stopped cold, tossed and shook his head, and pranced nervously. Animals on the prairie develop a profound respect for barbed wire. Each of them learns the lesson via deep cuts and torn skin. Beauty clearly saw the sweep of the line fence, and didn't comprehend that the wires had been lowered to let him step over. Barbed wire meant cuts and pain, whether it was lying on the ground or stretched tautly at one-, two- and three-foot heights.

I pulled the pony back and walked him around in a circle, as I had heard I should, and brought him up to the fence again with a tentative kick to his sides. Beauty stopped cold, shivering. Now both the horse and I were frightened.

I twisted around on the horse's back and looked back toward home, just as Brown reached the barns and turned to check our progress. He saw the situation immediately, cupped his hands and shouted as loudly as he could, "Kick him. Kick him."

I took a deep breath and dug the heels of my boots into the pony's sides. Beauty reared, then leaped forward, clearing the wire with a high, graceful leap. He left me sprawled on the ground, just missing falling on the wire. The horse galloped off across the range. I staggered to my feet, cap and lunchbox askew, frightened and hurting.

I looked back toward our house and barns and saw Mister Brown coming back out toward us. I stood there uncertainly, whimpering and pulling myself together. I guessed that Mister Brown would catch the horse and take him home. Since I wanted nothing more to do with that horse, I limped off toward the school.

At four o'clock when I emerged from the front door of the schoolhouse expecting a long walk home, there was Brown with Beauty.

"We're gonna try it a'gin, boy. It'll go OK this time. You just see."

I was scared and terribly embarrassed. By that time the rest of the children had gathered on the porch.

"What's goin' on, Howard? Your nurse come to getcha?

"He gonna carry you home, Howard? Can'tcha ride that little horse. Let's see ya ride him, Howard. You scared of that horse?"

I hadn't told anybody about the morning's problems, and none of the children had seen it. I had lived through an absolutely miserable day, couldn't study, and had been bawled out by the teacher for not being able to perform well at the blackboard in arithmetic class. I turned away and said nothing.

"C'mon, boy," Mister Brown said, trying to shorten up a bad situation. "Git aboard an' let's go."

I slung my lunchbox around my neck and under my arm. Mister Brown had brought the pony alongside the schoolhouse porch and I climbed aboard. The pony jerked his head upward and pranced, but Brown had a firm grip on the bridle and I stayed on. We started off along the roadside, following a fence until we could turn and head off across the prairie toward home, with Brown leading the pony but trying to keep out of the way as much as possible. I knew what was coming.

"Hey, he's leading the horse for Howard! Hey, Howard, that horse got you spooked? They gonna come and get you every day? How come your Mamma didn't come, too?"

I hung my head and gripped the horse's mane.

Brown and the pony kept steadily plodding along, and eventually the voices faded. The group on the schoolhouse porch broke up. The children started their separate ways home across the pastures and fields.

"Maybe I shouldn't 'a done that, boy. But, by golly, I thought you should git right back on that horse."

I said nothing. We plodded along, the horse settling down to the steady pace of the man holding the bridle.

When we came to the fence line, the horse again balked, stopped cold, trembling. I was fearfully gripping with my knees, holding my breath, expecting to be thrown again. The horse could feel the fear and uncertainty of its rider, and started to dance and shy sideways.

"OK, settle down, both of you," Brown said. "We're gonna do this right. You just relax, boy. Let up on those reins a little, an' don't hold him so tight with your knees and by his mane. Jes' loosen up, take it easy."

I was unsure and frightened. "Shouldn't I get down, Mister Brown?"

"Nossir, not on yer life. You an' this horse are gonna cross this little wire. Now, horse, stop that jumpin' around. Whasta matter with you. You seen lotsa fences, and this here fence ain't gonna hurt you. You jes' settle down, gol dern it, horse."

Brown stood in front of the horse, facing it, close, with a grip on the bit on either side of the horse's mouth. He was now talking soothingly, continuously to the horse. Beauty continued to tremble and dance. I hung on, too tight.

As he talked to the horse, Brown began to slowly back over the wire, moving very gently. Because of his closeness to the horse's head, Beauty couldn't see the wire on the ground, though he knew it was there. Brown kept slowly backing over the fence wire, and in a half-minute they were over.

The horse sensed they were over and relaxed. When the horse relaxed, I relaxed. Brown slowly stepped back from the horse's head. Beauty looked around warily at the fence, but stood still.

Brown walked forward beside the horse's head with one hand lightly holding one of the bridle reins near the bit. After a few paces, he let go of the bridle and looked up at me. "You ride him home, boy," he said. He stopped and waited for us to pass. Beauty skittered a little, but kept walking. I relaxed on the reins, and we made our way across the field to the barns. I jumped off, watered the horse, and put him in his stall in the barn.

Brown came over to see that everything was all right. "You OK, boy?"

I nodded. "Yup, thanks, Mister Brown."

"Wasn't no big thing, boy. Just somethin' that hadda be done. I hadda do something like that with circus animals lotsa times. Don't worry about it, boy."

But I did worry about it. I was ashamed and upset. I knew I had to ride the pony to school the next day. I knew there would be trouble at the fence. I knew I'd take a terrible teasing from the kids at school. I hardly slept at all that night. On Tuesday morning I was tired, groggy, and a little sick.

"Are you all right, Howard?" my Mother asked at breakfast.

"I'm OK," I said finally.

"It'll go all right with that horse now," my Dad said. I was silent.

The second day at the fence the horse shied and bucked and threw me again, but I hung on to one of the reins, and Beauty couldn't run away. I couldn't get back on, so I led the horse to school. The teasing was merciless when I got there. I kept my head down, my mouth shut, and took it. I didn't learn much in school that day.

On the way home the horse threw me again at the fence and got away from me. I caught it in the pasture and led it home. I saw Dad and Mister Brown watching, but when we got home they said nothing.

The third morning the horse bucked and jumped at the fence. Somehow I stayed on. I rode up to the schoolhouse in silent triumph. The jeering let up a little.

"That's a pretty nice horse," Freddie said at lunch time. "Can I ride him?"

I said "sure," and the experienced rider jumped on his smooth back and galloped the pony around and around the school yard and the surrounding prairie.

"He's a great horse, Howard. Rides like a rocking chair. Why don't you run him a little?"

I said nothing. So far I hadn't ridden Beauty faster than a brisk walk.

After school the horse and I started home at a slow, steady pace. I was holding the reins tight to keep the frisky pony from breaking into a run. Half way across an open stretch of prairie pasture the horse whinnied sharply, reared upward and backward, throwing me off in a heap, my lunchbox painfully crunching into my back. A big bullsnake was uncoiling and heading away from our line of travel. The pony galloped away about a quarter-mile, then stopped, the reins trailing at his front feet.

I dusted myself off and started after the pony, not really expecting to catch him. But Beauty stood shying and dancing, but holding his ground. I moved up to him steadily. The horse tossed his head and backed away a few steps. I finally reached out gently and caught one of the reins.

Beauty stood still while I came closer, hand over hand along the rein. When I was beside him, I patted the pony's neck. He bobbed his head, danced away a few steps, then the horse and I started walking home. There was no place for me to climb on him, so after a jumpy crossing of the downed fence, we walked the rest of the way home.

After that, Beauty and I slowly developed an understanding. There were more fall-offs and throw-offs. The pace of travel picked up from walking to a tight-rein trot, then to a little loping canter for short distances. By spring we were galloping smoothly across the pastures and fields, usually with a cautious, jumpy crossing of the fence line. I would give Beauty a gentle kick when we approached the fence to let him know he should keep moving and get it over with.

Brown watched us come home one afternoon, on an easy lope. He and my Dad were pitching hay over the fence to the feeder cattle. I heard them talking as I rode Beauty into the barn for his afternoon dressing.

"That boy finally got aholt of that horse, didn't he, Mister?" Brown asked.

"He did. You did a good job on that one, Brown. I appreciate it," Dad said.

Brown chuckled in acknowledgement of the compliment.

Probably, those were the kindest words that old man heard in the last years of his life. It was something good he could think about when he was gasping for life on a lonely, winter night in a hobo camp somewhere in Mississippi.

Model T

It crouched in the corner of our big machine shed like a giant cricket, buried in dust and straw. Burlap bags had been thrown over it years before. Dust covered everything, as well as a liberal layer of chicken manure from stray birds wandering in and resting there after scratching and feeding outside in the barnyards.

When Freddie Sanders and Johnny Bear came to visit, they would peek under the bags and examine the old engine. From under the coverings came an exciting aroma of old leather, enriched with a bouquet of stale grease and gasoline. It thrilled us to think someday it might run again. It was a 1919 Ford Touring Car. It had no top, just a windshield and two seats, a high back end and a rakish look. We never found out who it had belonged to, or how it got there. For some unknown reason my parents didn't want to discuss its genesis.

To me, in the years before I became thirteen, the mysterious old car was an obsession. I would ask Dad if he could pull it out of the shed and let me try to make it run.

"You're too young, Howard. You couldn't drive

it anyway. Just wait awhile," Dad would tell me.

At the beginning of the summer between my ninth and tenth grades, I again asked if we could pull out the old car and try to make it run. Dad said I could uncover it and clean it up if I worked on it evenings, Saturday afternoons and Sundays, so it would not interfere with my chores and my help with the field work.

I passed the word to Freddie and Johnny that I was going to try to resurrect the old Ford Roadster. The response was immediate. By July 4th, the car was virtually stripped to the frame. Every part that could be taken off or taken apart was removed, washed in gasoline until all the aged, dry grease and dirt was dissolved, then wiped clean. Slowly, sometimes working at night by lantern light in the big, gloomy machine shed, we began to reassemble it. After that summer, no automobile's anatomy was ever again a complete mystery to us — until the newest, computer-regulated cars were produced.

Two of the tires that had been propped up off the earthen floor were reasonably preserved. The tubes held air if not inflated too tightly. The other two tires were rotted and useless. We couldn't make them stay inflated. As the engine and running gear parts were slowly being re-assembled, we went out looking for tires that were no longer being manufactured.

There was also the problem of cash to buy the tires — if they could be found. So far the project had survived on the use of my Dad's hand tools, and gas stored for the farm tractor. Now, in addition to the two tires, there were a few simple parts needed that could be bought from any well-stocked auto junkyard.

We solved the immediate cash problem by talking Dad into letting us haul away a pile of old machinery parts and appliances that had assembled over the years, to sell for scrap metal. We borrowed Sanders' old truck, put in some of our tractor gas, added some used oil recently drained from the tractor, and hauled the scrap metal to the nearest junk metal dealer, thirty miles away. We got $14, and came home feeling flush.

Bob Jordahl was the used auto parts dealer in Groton. He was a greasy, disreputable man who never seemed to wash either his clothes or himself. He was so scroungy he seldom even went downtown, even to Hank's saloon, though he loved beer. He'd send one of his scrawny kids to get some bottles of beer when he had any money. We didn't remember ever seeing a woman around the shacky, unpainted house surrounded by wrecked cars, piles of parts, and weeds, but there must have been one.

The wrecked or abandoned cars he took the parts from came from unknown sources, mostly at night, it seemed. But Bob had two tires to fit the old Model T Ford, and he knew they were valuable. He knew about the project of starting up the old Ford at the Jones's place, and we also suspected he knew how much money we had.

As the leader of the project, and the nominal owner of both the car and the money, I tried to deal with him first. Freddie was with me. Bob said he wasn't interested in selling at any price. He noted that we couldn't keep our eyes off the two tires leaning against the back wall of his parts shack. We went away in deep depression, with no tires.

We recruited Ralph Sanders, Freddie's older brother, to try to make a deal for the tires. Ralph tried him the next Saturday night. He got closer. He got Bob to give him a price: $12 — $6 apiece. Too much. Ralph went downtown and told us it looked pretty tough. Maybe we'd have to pay him the twelve dollars.

Deno stopped by our house the next Saturday afternoon to see how the project was progressing. Deno loved cars. He would have been glad to pitch in and finish the job for us at any stage, but he knew it was our show and he didn't even give us much advice, even though he was a super mechanic. He offered to tune up the electrical system when the time came. We told him about the trouble with Bob and the tires.

Gossip had it that Deno was a rural bootlegger in the late 1920's. The word around the country was that he had been plenty tough. He was an affable, helpful person now, but we heard that he had been through a number of violent adventures hauling booze over from the stills in Stearns County, Minnesota. He had been caught and arrested a few times when he was unable to outrun or out-maneuver the various sheriffs or federal agents along his routes. They said he never stayed in jail more than a day or so.

Deno was a member of a large and prominent family relationship in Brown County. No Brown County sheriff, or even a sheriff from a neighboring county, wanted to put Deno in the poky for more than a day or two. If Deno's relatives got riled at the sheriff, he almost certainly wouldn't get re-elected.

When he heard about the problem with the tires, Deno said, "Boys, meet me in town tonight, and we'll go see that S.O.B. I'll get your tires. Bring your money."

That evening we drove up to the junkyard in Deno's purring, almost-new car. Deno didn't waste any time or words.

"Listen, you bastard, you sell these kids them tires at the right price or I'll send some boys over here to beat the shit outa you."

"Jeesus, Deno, what the hell's the matter with you?" Bob said loudly, his bravado still in place. "Wadda ya mean, drivin' up here to my place of business an' threatenin' me? I'm a businessman. I got a livin' to make. You don't walk in to Harvey at the hardware store an' tell him what he can sell, an' at what price. Who the hell you think you are?"

"Lissen, you ain't no businessman," Deno growled. "You're a goddam thief. You stole most of them parts an' cars, an' everybody knows it. You raise your voice to me an' I'll start talking about where some of them parts an' cars came from. I know, and you know I know. So sell them kids them tires for $3 apiece or this goddam junk yard is goin' to be a piece of plowed ground, right after I burn it clean to the ground."

"Shit, damn, Deno." Bob was beginning to waver. "You ain't so big. How do you get off talking so tough?"

"I am tough," Deno said softly. "An' I got some guys backing me up that makes me look like a cream puff. You've seen Tuffy and them other boys work over smart guys from out of town."

"Well, I was gonna sell them kids them tires, but I wasn't gonna give 'em away." Bob's voice had taken on more of its habitual whine. "Jesus, Deno, let me make a buck, for God's sake."

"You'll make a buck, you turd. You stole them tires anyway."

"I'll sell 'em both tires an' tubes for seven bucks."

"You got a deal," Deno said. "An' I'll bring you a beer later from Hank's Place. Give him the seven bucks, kids."

So we learned how some adults conducted business and we got the tires.

A week or so later the car project was getting pretty exciting. With the "new" tires on, and the other two patched and holding air, it looked pretty good. It was being steadily re-assembled. There weren't any parts left over. We cranked the engine "dry," without any gas or oil in it, and the parts seemed to mesh and turn the way they were supposed to.

We were afraid to try to start it. What if, after a summer's work, it wouldn't run? We leaned on it, patted it, and discussed over and over each step. Had we done anything wrong? Had we lost anything, left anything off? Eventually we had to try it.

We decided to try to start it on the third Sunday afternoon in August. We pushed it out of the shed into the yard and stood admiring it.

"She's beautiful," Johnny Bear said. "She looks great!"

Freddie, who knew the most about cars, sat behind the wheel fiddling with the spark and gas levers, snapping the "key" on and off.

"Gas 'n water 'n oil OK?" Freddie asked.

"All OK," I answered. "You got to crank it, Johnny. Remember I busted my wrist a couple of months ago."

"Boy. I'm not so sure. I hear those engines really can kick back. You got your arm busted cranking the tractor. I don't want mine broke cranking this darn Ford."

"Aw, c'mon, Johnny," Freddie said. "You ain't gonna be spooked by this little old engine, are you?"

Johnny Bear stood by the crank and thought about it for a few moments. "OK, I'll try it."

Tentatively, he approached the crank and turned it over slowly.

"You gotta crank her harder than that," Freddie called from behind the wheel. "You ain't got enough speed on that crank to get a spark from the magneto."

Johnny stopped cranking and straightened up. "You crank it if you know so much."

"Aw, c'mon, Johnny, I didn't mean nothin'. Give her a couple of quick turns."

Johnny took a deep breath, hesitated, then spun the crank around for three quick turns. Nothing happened except a little foam of gas and air showed up where the gas line made a connection with the carburetor.

"We're bringing up some gas," I sang out. "but it won't fire. Maybe the magneto doesn't work and there is no spark."

"Let's try putting just a little gas in at the top of the carburetor," Freddie said. "If that doesn't work, we'll check the spark."

I put a few ounces of gas in the top of the carburetor.

"Give it a try, Johnny," I said.

Johnny stepped up to the crank, with more confidence now, hesitated a second, then started to spin the crank. There was a pop, a kind of backfire. Johnny jumped back from the front of the car, and suddenly it was running, making the popping, rattling sound of a badly-timed, four-cylinder engine.

It ran for about thirty or forty explosions. Johnny started jumping up and down, waving his arms, his mouth working but no sound coming out. I stood with my mouth open, frozen, gaping at the wildly vibrating engine. Freddie was hysterically working the gas and spark levers on the steering column, trying to keep it running. It died. There was silence for a few seconds.

"Jeesus Christ," Freddie said in an unreal, high-pitched voice. "It ran. It goddam ran."

Then all three of us were jumping up and down, shouting and laughing.

"It's gonna run," Freddie said. "It's sure gonna run. We musta got her back together right. We just gotta get used to her. We've gotta fix the timing. We gotta go see Deno."

"Let's try it again. Let's make sure it will run first," I said.

We kept walking around the car. We couldn't stand still.

"It's gonna run. It's gonna run," Johnny was repeating half to himself.

"Put in a little more gas on top and I'll try to set the gas and spark better," Freddie said.

This time Johnny stepped right up to the crank.

"Be careful, Johnny. Don't hook your thumb over the crank. It could still kick you," I cautioned

Sure enough, on the second turn of the crank, the engine fired early. The crank spun backward in a blur of motion. Fortunately, Johnny was quick and yanked his hand away almost fast enough. The spinning crank just caught a knuckle and knocked off the skin.

"You OK, Johnny?" He looked startled.

"Yeah. That thing is fast, though," he said.

"Want to try it again?"

"Not today. My luck just ran out."

I wanted to see the engine run again. I thought a few seconds about having two broken wrists in one year, then curiosity and excitement overcame caution.

"I'll do it with my left hand," I said.

I took a jump-back stance, as if batting against a wild fast-baller, and looked at Freddie. He nodded.

I spun the crank and the engine started. It must have run for fifteen or twenty seconds, popping loudly, backfiring and vibrating as if it was going to leap away from its mountings. Then it quit.

"She's way out of timing, but she runs," Freddie said quietly.

Just then my Dad walked up to the machine shed door. He had heard the racket and seen the excitement.

"It runs, Dad," I said.

He chuckled and nodded. "I heard," he said.

I felt hot tears in my eyes.

Freddie and I decided to immediately ride our bikes to Deno's farm while Johnny Bear headed for home on his horse. It was dark when we got there. Deno opened his kitchen door and, with his lop-sided grin, looked curiously at two tired boys.

"She runs, Deno," Freddie said. "But she's way out of time."

"You crazy goddam kids," Deno said, still grinning. "You really done something, didn't you. I sure hope you don't kill yourselves with that thing." After a pause, "I'll stop by tomorrow night and set the timing on it. Just leave her sit 'til I get there."

Thus started a saga that carried on through high school. The Model T figured into many of our adventures during a happy time of our lives.

Goin' fishin' with the Model T.

Goose for Supper

Wayne Bautista came to school with the news that there was a giant flock of maybe a thousand wild Canada geese in the Putney Slough. He said he had watched them from about a half-mile away after school the night before, circling and honking as they came in from feeding in the grain fields and gradually settling down for the night.

He said on the way to school in the morning, that he had watched again as they moved out of the slough to feed in the harvested fields, gleaning the hundreds of bushels of grain left by the grain combines and corn pickers.

In front of our lockers in the upstairs hallway, Manley Green, Don Woods and I listened to the report, glanced at each other and moved off for a quick conference.

"We gotta get a crack at those geese. That flock is gonna move out in a day or two, maybe tomorrow morning. If we don't get out there, we're goin' to be sorry," Manley said.

"Yeah, We can't pass this one up. It may be the last big flock we see this fall," I said. "You think we should take off now?"

Don Wood broke in, conservative as usual. "We can't take off now. Everybody has seen us here, even the teachers. We'd really get busted if everybody knew we took off to go goose hunting."

"Right after school then, right at four o'clock," Manley decided.

"What about football practice?" I asked.

"We're gonna miss it."

"We'll catch more hell for missing football practice than we will for skipping school. Old Coach Doney's just goin' to blow his stack. He'll really go crazy."

"Yeah, but he can't kick us out of school, an' he probably won't throw us off the football team. I think it's worth the hell we're gonna get," Manley decided.

"It's goin' to be bad," Don said, "but probably not as bad as missing getting a shot or two at that flock of geese."

At noon hour we quickly left the school by a side door to gather guns, boots and ammunition, and stow them in my Grandmother's garage, near where the Model T was parked.

Some of the other junior and senior boys suspected what was up.

"You guys happen to be goin' huntin'?" a teammate asked. "You planning to maybe miss football practice? You think Doney won't know where you went to? Man, you guys are gonna get burned!"

"What are you talking about? Where'd you get that crazy idea about goose hunting? Tell you what," Don said. "Just don't go out of your way to get us into trouble, an' we'll do the same for you sometime, okay?"

We all went off to afternoon classes. The last hour dragged slowly by. When the bell rang, we three boys moved swiftly through the milling students, slipped out the side door and sprinted the four blocks to where the Model T was parked.

"This darned thing better start. We gotta get out of town and out of sight as fast as we can. That coach is gonna be pretty mad," Manley puffed.

Don was frantically spinning the crank, while I worked the levers on the steering column. The Model T coughed, caught, and came to an uncertain, rattling life. We jumped in and headed out of town by back streets and an obscure dirt road.

Putney Slough was about seven miles northwest of Groton, an irregularly shaped backwater of the James River, surrounded on three sides by farmland and pasture, and on the fourth side by the river. It had been a warm, dry summer. The open water in the slough had retreated about fifty to a hundred yards in from each edge of the slough. The edges were areas of muddy, mucky ground, with occasional grass hummocks providing an opportunity to climb out of the slime.

We decided the best approach would be to crawl up from the south side, get as close as possible to the open water and the resting flock of geese. As we parked the car and watched, smaller flocks were rising from the water, squawking and honking as they circled to scout for danger and gain altitude, then they would swing out away from the slough to land several miles away in one of the grain fields to feed. If we could get close enough, we could get in some shots at the birds swinging out and returning, when they were still near enough to the ground for the buck shot to penetrate their dense feathers, or break a wing, to bring down the heavy birds.

To get to the south edge of the slough, we would have to cross a half-mile of Alberts' big pasture, which held a small herd of dairy and beef cattle. Sometimes

Mr. Alberts would release his big Holstein bull to mingle with the cows for obvious reasons. Today was one of those days. We didn't see the giant bull until we were well out in the pasture heading for the slough. We were wearing hip boots, carrying guns, ammunition and decoys, and in no condition to out-run an angry bull and roll under the fence to safety.

The huge animal broke away from the herd and advanced toward us at a lumbering trot, growling and bawling as he came. We froze.

"Jeez," Manley breathed. "What the dickens are we gonna do?"

"Run!" I gasped.

"We'll never make it to the fence!"

"Shoot him!"

"We can't do that. We can't kill that bull. Mr. Alberts would go out of his mind."

"Why not? That bull's goin' to kill us!"

"Let's split up. Run three ways. He can't get all of us."

"Adios," Donny said, and dashed for the west fence.

"Bye," Manley said, and he took off east, toward the other fence.

I stood there, alone, watching the big bull lumbering toward me. I couldn't make my legs move. My mouth dropped open in a silent scream. The bull thundered to a stop ten yards from me, and stood with head down, bawling hoarsely, beginning to paw the soft earth, flinging it behind him in a long arc. He was gathering himself to charge.

Donny, now half-way to the fence, stopped, turned and shouted, "The tree. Go to the tree. It's behind you. Back up slow."

I turned my head slowly, slightly breaking my eye-lock with the slavering bull. From the edge of my field of vision a stark, dead cottonwood, with branches eight to ten feet from the ground appeared. Turning back to the snorting, growling bull, I again locked eyes with him, then slowly leaned forward and dropped my shotgun to the ground. Then I dropped a gray, canvas bag I was carrying that held slats to build a blind if one was needed. I backed slowly away.

The bull advanced to the bundle, lowering his head. With the ugly, curved horns, he nudged the bundle, then tossed it in the air with a great upward arching of his neck and body, coming down with his hooves on my precious shotgun. In that instant I speeded up my retreat, and when the bull looked for me, I was nearly at the tree. The animal came in a full, galloping charge. I sprinted for the tree, ducked behind it and desperately leaped for the lowest limb. I caught it, swung my feet up to catch another branch, and hung suspended, face upward, eight feet off the ground.

The bull could have reared up and hooked me down, but he hesitated, maybe confused by the way I had disappeared into the air. This gave me time. With a great muscular effort I could never again duplicate, I twisted my way around the limb and clawed my way further up the tree, out of reach.

The bull stood pawing and snorting, saliva drooling from his open, bawling mouth, looking up at me with reddened eyes. I stood on a branch, clinging to the trunk of the tree, my body suddenly so weak and trembling I was afraid I might fall.

"Way to go, Howard. Great show!" Manley shouted from the east fence. He was laughing. I looked down at the enraged animal, wanting to kill him, then looked out west to where Donny was close to the safety of that fence. Donny waved and smiled. I wanted to vomit — and did — on the bull's upturned face.

I heard Manley roar with laughter, then watched with wonder as he gathered his gun and ammunition and headed for the slough. Donny saw Manley's move and also began working his way toward the geese. "Keep him busy, Howard," he shouted. "We'll want to come back your way."

I swore at the bull, at my friends and at the sky, and watched them go. The stand-off at the tree continued for fifteen minutes, then a half-hour. I watched Donny and Manley disappear into the rushes at the edge of the swamp. The bull began to get bored, wavered in his baleful watch of me, and gave up pawing the earth at the base of the tree. I had consolidated my position in the sturdy cottonwood, stopped shaking and rested, seething with anger.

From my high vantage perch, I saw a flock of about thirty geese rise from the center of the slough, circle around and head out almost exactly between the points where Donny and Manley had disappeared. Then I heard four shots, carefully paced, by hunters who knew how to shoot. The flock flared sharply, turning frantically back toward the open water, but two beautiful geese spun earthward and disappeared into the high grass.

The shots spooked the bull. He didn't run, but he broke his vigil at the tree and started to amble back to the herd of cows near the farm buildings. I held my place, watching the animal move away. When I looked back toward the slough, I saw my friends emerge, each holding high a big honker by the neck. They moved along the west fence and began to work their way toward the road and the car.

I didn't want to shout and remind the bull I was still there. I watched the triumphant hunters move happily along, gesturing to each other and occasionally looking toward the tree where I was fuming on my perch. The bull slowly maintained its course away from the tree.

The boys at the fence waved for me to come over. I thought about it awhile, then slowly worked my way down the branches, and finally dropped to the ground, watching my adversary continue to move away. I walked cautiously to the torn bundle and broken shotgun, picked them up and started at a quickening pace toward the boys and the fence.

They held up the geese as I approached. "Nice birds, really big," Donny grinned.

I was silent, lips compressed. I dropped my broken gun and torn bundle over the fence and crawled under.

"Aw, c'mon, Howard," Donny said. "You gotta admit it was kinda funny."

"That big bastard was trying to kill me. That wasn't funny. You guys got a weird sense of humor."

"We also got two geese," Manley said.

"What about a goose for me?"

"Well, they're pretty well spooked now. The whole flock took off when we shot. Maybe we could come out again in the morning."

"Yeah, Manley will handle the bull tomorrow," Donny said.

We chugged quietly back to town, again using back roads and side streets. We drove the Model T into the alley behind my grandmother's house. The six o'clock siren on the water tower was moaning over the town as the motor died.

We had already field-dressed the two geese in the roadside ditch near the slough. "How we gonna get these birds home? Can't just drag 'em through town." Donny said.

"You can hang 'em in Grandma's garage until after dark," I said. "If I haven't decided to clean 'em and take them inside, you can pick 'em up."

"Lissen, Howard. I'll give you and your Grandma half my goose. It's a big bird, an' there's a meal in it for two families," Donny offered.

"We better stop worrying about them geese an' start worrying about what Ol' Coach Doney's gonna do to us. We might be ex-football players right now," Manley warned.

"Aw, I think he needs us. He'll just be really mad, an' scream an' holler at us," I said. "We need a good story for him, though."

The next morning Coach Doney was waiting on the front steps of the school when I approached. The coach stared me down until we were practically nose to nose.

"Come down to the locker room," he said coldly.

"Got to go to class, Coach."

"Are you telling me what you are going to do? Did somebody tell you that you were running this school?" The color was rising in the coach's face, turning it purplish red. I saw the veins pop out on his neck and forehead.

"No, Sir." I went past him down the hall and down the stairs to the locker room. Donny and Manley were already there, sitting silently on the bench in front of their lockers. I joined them.

"I guess you big shots think you can come and go as you please," the coach said. "I guess you think you know more about coaching a football team than I do. I guess you think you are so wonderful you don't have to practice, that you decide when you feel like practicing. Let the other guys practice and carry you three deadbeats like three bags of blubber." He was warming up to his tirade, his face again bright red, veins and eyes bulging.

We hunched down and took it, as the speed and crescendo of his wrath grew. Finally, after another minute of nearly uncontrolled rage, he stopped, then said, "Much as I hate to inquire into your important personal affairs, where were you guys anyway, while the rest of us were trying to figure out how to fill in for your jobs on the football team, and to give you a free ride when you eventually decided to show up?"

"We had an emergency with some cattle," Manley said.

"What cattle? What emergency? You loafers don't handle any cattle!"

"Well, there was a problem with a bull. Howard's the only one who knows how to handle him. Donny and me had to help, to see that he didn't get hurt. It was a difficult situation."

Just then the bell rang loudly, signaling the start of the first class. We stood up. Doney knew he couldn't keep us from class, and he had his own class to teach.

"Bull!" he shouted. "I'll bet there was bull! You guys can go and chase bulls Friday night. You're not playing on my football team."

"What about after that?" Donny asked.

"We'll see about 'after that.' We'll see if there are any more bull problems. We'll see if you deadbeats are willing to practice a few extra hours."

We quickly climbed the stairs to classroom level.

"No lies, we told no lies," Manley said, as we hurried down the hall.

"Bull," I growled.

Saturday Night

In the summer between our junior and senior years in high school, we were beginning to grow up, we thought. We were doing men's work on our respective farms, and occasionally on Saturday nights we were allowed to go to the pavilion dances. Of course we drove the Model T, sometimes making the complete round trip without a flat tire.

Any of the young people in the neighborhood who were old enough, and who didn't happen to have dates, were welcome to ride along. Neither Freddie, nor Johnny Bear, nor I had regular girl friends. Sometimes we would meet former girlfriends at the dances, and there would be some hugging and kissing among the trees along the river that flowed just behind the pavilion in the park.

On a hot Saturday in August, in the midst of a better-than-usual harvest, word got to the kids in the neighborhood that the Model T was going to attempt the fourteen miles to Armandale Park where there was a dance in the pavilion. After a quick supper, with the sun still a couple of hours above the horizon, I filled the Model T's radiator with water at the stock trough, pulled over to the barrels by the machine shed and filled the tank with tractor gas, then took the tire pump from under the front seat and added a few strokes of air to the right front tire.

I went to the standpipe, washed my hands again, pulled on a clean T-shirt, cranked the car and headed down the road to the Sanders farm. Freddie and his sisters, Doris and Edith, were waiting outside the front door.

"Doris and Edith both want to go. S'pose there's enough room?" Freddie called to me over the noise of the engine.

I turned off the engine. "'Course there's room. We got room for as many kids as the tires will hold up."

"What about the Bensons?" Doris asked.

"We'll take anybody that want's to go, or as many as we can get aboard."

"OK, we're goin'," Doris said. "Just give us a few minutes to get ready."

Freddie's sisters were lively, good-looking, sturdy girls who loved to laugh and dance. Although they were smart kids, getting good grades in school wasn't important to them. What was important was getting along, having a good time, and eventually getting married and having children of their own.

Freddie, his parents, three sisters, two older brothers and younger twin brothers lived in a comfortable, ramshackle, weather-beaten house that hadn't seen a coat of paint in two generations of Sanders. Ivy, the mother, was fat, jolly and a great cook, who celebrated every day with her children as another triumph of survival. Roy, the father, ordinarily observed the whole family quietly, seeming to enjoy and endure the triumphs and tragedies with equanimity. Roy didn't work much; Ivy and the children provided most of the labor for the farm. Roy provided a gentle, passive direction, and watched to see that things didn't go too far wrong.

The Sanders were a strong presence in the neighborhood and the school, not leaders, but popular, interesting people to have around. They had the first radio in the community, a cumbersome affair hooked up to a series of car batteries, with a long wire aerial strung high between two poles in their front yard. When we were in the lower grades at the country school, Freddie had invited me and Johnny Bear to stay over and listen to "Gang Busters" and "Amos 'n' Andy". It was a fabulous experience, carrying us away, briefly, from the grimness of the drought and depression on the prairie.

Freddie and I waited a half-hour in the shadow of Sander's farmyard trees while the girls washed, fussed and primped.

Freddie went to the door and called to the bustle going on inside. "C'mon you girls. We aren't goin' to wait any longer. Let's crank her up, Howard."

Just as the engine crackled to life, the two girls came running for the car and jumped into the back seat. The noisy load in the car took off for Benson's, all four of us laughing and chattering over the racket and rattle of the car.

Phyllis and Doraine Benson were ready to go, standing on the front porch of the rambling farmhouse with their mother.

"Have you got enough room?" Phyllis called.

I left the motor running and called back over the racket, "We've always got enough room for you girls. Hop in."

The girls climbed aboard, one in front and one in back. Mrs. Benson came over to my side of the car and rested her hands on the vibrating machine. "You'll be careful, won't you, Howard?"

"Oh, sure, Mrs. Benson. This thing won't go fast

enough to hurt anybody. But I'll be careful."

She backed away, smiled, and waved at us as we chugged down the driveway, laughing with the excitement of getting away from the isolated farms for a few hours.

Johnny was waiting at the corner, having walked nearly a mile from his house to save us some time, and wear on the frail tires.

"Where you guys been? I was about ready to walk to the park."

"Jump in, Johnny," Doraine called.

"Where?"

"Anywhere. How about you sittin' up on the back of the back seat?"

"OK, OK!" Grinning, he climbed over the rear of the car and perched on the back of the back seat.

"This thing actually goin' to get there?" he asked me.

"Always has before. Hang on. Here we go!"

It took us over a half-hour to go the remaining eleven miles to the park. I didn't want to drive very fast because it would put an extra strain on the puny tires. It was easier to go slowly than to patch a tire. Anyway, we were having almost as much fun driving through the cooling twilight as we would when we got there.

It was nearly dark, and the small band was in full volume when we arrived at the pavilion, parked in the trees, and paid twenty-five cents each to have our hands stamped for admission.

Everyone was having a great time. The pavilion and the surrounding park was scattered with classmates from the high school. After the long summer, we were glad to see each other. There were plenty of slaps on the back and punches on the arm between the boys, friendly waves and greetings, whispers and giggles, and a few warm embraces between girls and guys.

There was some beer circulating in the shadows among the trees, and some schnapps. It was quietly passed around, and slowly consumed. There wasn't enough for anyone to get drunk. At midnight the band stopped, and people began to assemble by their cars. Phyllis and I had been dancing together nearly all the time, and faded into the woods on two occasions for some kisses. This didn't go unnoticed by Freddie and Johnny Bear.

They got together by the Model T. When we got to the car Johnny said, "Why don't I drive? You can sit with Phyllis, an' Freddie can entertain the rest of the girls."

"How about you?" Freddie asked.

"Aw, I'm out of it. You know that. I'll drive."

"Well, let me bring it around to the road," Freddie said.

"No, I'll do it, Freddie."

The other kids were milling about the car, saying goodnight, talking and laughing. Somebody spun the crank on the Model T, and a big cheer went up when it coughed into life.

There are three floorboard foot pedals in a Model T Ford — brake, low gear and reverse.

In the dark, nobody was sure who was behind the wheel. Whoever it was touched the wrong pedal, and instead of moving forward, out toward the driveway, the car moved quickly backward and its high back crunched against a tree. Simultaneously, there was a high, choking scream.

Instantly the car moved forward. Everybody jumped out and ran to the rear. On the ground, writhing and gasping, was Jane Ryan. For a moment everybody froze, then gasps turned to screams by the girls.

An older boy dropped to his knees by the fallen girl and tried to see the extent of her injury. The park ranger who had been near, observing the departures, came running over with his flashlight. He knelt by the girl.

"Jane, can you speak to me?" he said softly. She continued to writhe and moan.

There were screams of anguish, long keening shrieks as the Benson and Sanders girls clung to each other, trembling and crying hysterically. Randy Ryan, Jane's brother, was on his knees by her, pale, shaking, and praying. The grief-stricken crowd around the crushed girl soon included everyone still in the park. The pavilion manager had already called the Sheriff's Office. A sheriff's car and a doctor were on the way. The ranger determined there was no major external bleeding. Someone came with a blanket. He covered her with it and carefully tucked it in around her.

For the sobbing, shattered crowd, the wait for the doctor seemed endless. Attention began to turn to the circumstances of the accident.

"Who did it? Who was driving?" asked one of the boys, not of the Groton High School group. When he didn't receive an answer, he took Freddie Sanders by the arm. "Who did it? Who was driving?" he asked again.

Freddie pulled his arm away roughly, glaring at the intruder. "None of your business. Keep out of this," he said harshly.

The other boy was shocked and hurt by his abrupt exclusion from the Groton group. "Well, somebody's at fault. Isn't anybody going to find out who hurt her?"

The Groton group was silent. Freddie, Johnny and I, standing close to the girls, were in numbed shock. Nobody spoke. Randy Ryan was still on his knees by his sister, sobbing. Some friends were kneeling with him, trying to comfort him.

Time dragged horribly until we saw the flashing light of the sheriff's car. The young emergency room doctor from the only hospital within thirty miles jumped out to kneel by the girl. The ranger held the flashlight while the doctor made a quick examination.

The doctor turned away from her to talk to the deputy. "I can't tell the exact extent of her injuries," he said. "Some broken bones for sure, maybe internal injuries."

Jane was still conscious. He spoke to her gently. "You're going to pull through. We're going to take you to the hospital and patch you up. I'm going to bandage you up as best I can right here, very quickly."

The Deputy went into the pavilion office and used the phone. "The ambulance is right behind us," he told the doctor. "Ambulance" in this case was a hearse with some oxygen and medical equipment and supplies. There wasn't a fully equipped ambulance within two hundred miles. The doctor continued to work on the injured girl.

"I'm going to have to ask some questions," the deputy announced softly to the group. "Whose car is this?"

"It's mine." I stepped forward.

"Were you driving?"

"No."

"Who was?"

"I don't know."

"You don't know?"

"I wasn't near the car when it happened."

"Who was? Who was driving?"

"I don't know."

The deputy paused and looked around the group. "All right, we're not going to get this done here." He paused. "I'll just get the names of the people involved with the car, and we'll get at the other questions tomorrow."

After he had the names, he closed his notebook and took a deep breath. "I will follow Randy home and talk to Jane's parents. Doc, I assume you will ride back to Aberdeen with Jane?"

The doctor nodded without looking up from his bandaging.

The deputy looked carefully at me, Freddie and Johnny. "After the ambulance comes, you can drive that thing home."

It was a long, silent, sad trip home. Each group had to wake up their parents and tell them about the accident. There were endless questions, always ending with, "But who was driving?"

"I don't know."

"You don't know?"

Silence.

In the days following the accident, the community was overwhelmed with shock and sorrow. The families involved were very close. They suffered the concern almost equally with the immediate family of Jane. Word from the hospital was that she would live, but possibly be permanently crippled.

Not much was said about who was at the controls of the Model T for a few days. We were told that the sheriff had a discussion with Jim Ryan, Jane's father, asking him if he wanted an investigation or to press charges against anyone.

"Oh God, Marvin, we don't want to get into that! I don't want to drag it out. Everybody is so sick about it, it would be hell to have to talk about it. Let's leave it alone."

"All right, Jim," Marvin said quietly. "I don't

believe there was a specific crime, just a terrible accident. Later, if you want me to follow up on it, I'll do it."

The tears were welling up again in Jim's eyes and coursing down his haggard face. "No, Marvin, let's leave it alone. Nobody wanted to hurt Jane."

Marvin touched him on the arm. "So long, Jim. I'm so sorry." He got into his car and drove out of the yard and away.

Some others in the community didn't want to forget about it. Motivated by warped righteousness, they raised the cry to find out who accidentally touched the reverse pedal and crushed Jane Ryan. Freddie, Johnny and I were silent about it.

The tempo of the gossip picked up when the fall term started at the high school. In a group by Hank's saloon on a Saturday night in late September, someone declared loudly, "I think that Indian kid done it. Them Indians can't handle liquor, you know. There was liquor out there. He got drunk and backed into Janey."

Some other loud mouths picked up his refrain. Someone reminded the listeners that Freddie Sanders was also near the front of the car, but a couple of Freddie's brothers were there and that subject was dropped. Other boys had been in the area. I wasn't considered a suspect. I had been smooching with Phyllis in the trees.

Over the weeks the gossip continued. We heard about all of it and remained silent.

One Sunday evening in late October, a parade of six cars drove slowly past the Bear-Day farmhouse, horns honking. Shouts came from the open windows. "Drunk Indian! Get out of here, you stinkin' Indians."

Johnny ran into the yard. John Bear was already there facing the road. Together, they silently stared down the ugly parade. On the second pass the drivers threw bags of garbage at the fence and drove away.

Jim Ryan heard about it the next day. We were told he hurried over to the Bear-Day place. He talked to John Bear in the yard. "I'm sorry about what happened last night. I'm sick about it. I had nothing to do with it, John."

"It's OK, Jim. I know you wasn't involved. It's OK, don't worry about it. Them people will cool off after a while," he said without conviction.

Johnny Bear wasn't at school on Monday. The football coach was frantic. Johnny was his star.

"Where is he?" he thundered at me.

"I don't know Coach. You know what happened."

"That shouldn't scare him off. He's not a weakling. He's got to show up. We need him."

"Somebody should have told that to the guys who were screaming at his family and throwing garbage in his yard."

"Don't get smart with me," the coach roared, and shook his fist at me.

"Where is he, Freddie?" the coach demanded.

Freddie just shook his head and didn't answer.

Johnny Bear was never seen at the high school again. In a few weeks I got a brief letter:

> *Dear Howard,*
> *I joined the Marines. Going to California for training. Good luck.*
> *J.*

The Groton football team lost its final two games.

Spring

In the spring in the Dakotas, when it rains, everything is forgiven The land is wonderful, soft, loving and kind. The delicious smell of the blend of rich, moist earth, wild flowers and other growing things overwhelms the senses. It blows you away, it is so beautiful.

In the spring of l942, the harsh agonies of the last ten years were forgotten. Somehow the sturdiest families had endured. They were still there on the land, looking forward to lush green fields, rich harvests, and crisp, cold, restorative winters with snow covering the land instead of drifts of blowing dust.

The land was beginning to heal itself with the return of moderate rainfall. It was also getting a lot of help from the people who had stayed with it, respected it, cared for it. The Government had provided tree seedlings to farmers who contracted to place them in rows to form windbreaks across the flat land. The hardy trees that were cared for caught on, and islands of growing green were beginning to replace the ridges of dust mixed with tumbleweeds that had been the main features of the flat land.

The plows were steadily throwing the drifted dirt

back from the dust dunes and fence rows. The fields were beginning to look normal, cared for.

A lesson had been learned, quickly by the progressive farmers, more slowly by some others. The lesson was that the land must be cared for. It had been abused and exploited by the early settlers, the land barons and bonanza farmers, just a generation ahead of the dust bowl families.

Maybe it was the natural progression of things, meant to be so. The early ones found the land, broke it up and made it bountiful — too bountiful. The next generation learned, almost too late, that the land couldn't bear merciless exploitation and abuse. They were developing a rudimentary care system, crude but a start.

It was up to the third generation, us and those to follow, to build the dams, contour the fields to slow down the erosion, learn to properly rotate crops and restore fertility, to use both chemical and natural fertilizer wisely to rebuild the soil. The great dams on the Missouri River that may have been castigated as political boondoggles at the time they were built, saved the life of the Dakota prairie.

In the days before the "Great Lakes of the Missouri," the prevailing northwest winds would leave the Pacific Coast area loaded with moisture. A lot of it would be lost as the air passed over the Rocky Mountains, but the wind was still a viable carrier of moisture as it swept across Montana and Wyoming. But there had been no restoration of moisture when the flowing air hit the Great Plains. The winds were drained and dried while passing over the hundreds of miles of flatland east of the Rockies. The cloud banks would dissolve and dissipate in the dry air, and by the time they reached the Dakotas, Nebraska and Kansas, there was nothing left to give.

A new movement had started with individual farmers, laboriously building dikes and dams across creek beds and sloughs to form small, artificial lakes, ponds and "tanks." These water places made a contribution not only to the livestock and the growing things around them, but also to the air above them, helping to restore its moisture as it swept across the land. Work that had started with doubt and desperation was beginning to pay off. The land was bursting into life that spring of l942.

In the school, students were responding to the marvelous re-generation of the prairie. The long winter was transformed into an exciting world of music contests, track meets, boys and girls, proms and graduation.

The track men started running in March while there were still snowdrifts, slush and mud. We didn't run on the athletic fields or on the track. In the mud and muck we would have ruined them. So we ran the country roads, mile after exhausting mile. After football in the fall, athletic activity became pretty slow for those of us who didn't play basketball. There was a little wrestling and boxing, gym class and intramural basketball, but not the hard, grinding workout that kept young bodies in good condition. We found we were in terrible shape.

The first five-mile run nearly killed me. We were running in packs of four or five. The seniors were up ahead, as was proper. We were horsing around, showing off — bigger and stronger than the younger boys, so our status put us in front.

The first mile was fun. Great to be outside the stuffy school building into the fresh, raw, early spring air. The sweat suits gave off a heady smell of mothballs and wintergreen. We were wearing bulky overshoes over our gym shoes or tennis shoes, those that had them. Those that didn't, wore their regular winter footwear to slog through the snow and slush. Whatever we wore, they were heavy for running.

They were supposed to be heavy. Coach Doney's philosophy of training was to drive one's self all out, as far as one could go, every day. Give maximum exertion over a period of time and the body will condition itself. If you survived, you made the team, or at least qualified for it. If you dropped out, you could get another chance, providing you kept going all out until you couldn't go any further.

So, after two weeks of workouts in the gym, exercises and stretching, and hundreds of laps around the basketball floor, we were supposedly ready for our first five-mile outdoor run. Everyone had to run to get in shape — dash runners, distance runners, high jumpers, shot putters, hurdlers — everyone. As a matter of fact, most of the track and field athletes participated in two or three events; there wasn't the specialization as in college or Olympic competition. There were shot putters who ran dashes and milers who were high jumpers.

I had hurt my leg in football the fall before in the second to last game, a hair-line fracture, so I had taken it easy that winter. I had hung around with the "brains" and girls after school instead of being involved in athletic programs. It had been a fun winter. Lots of new things to try out, new thoughts, and new types of relationships, but a terrible way to stay in good physical condition. So I had to get in shape the hard way.

The net culmination of all this agony, suffering, sacrifice and exhaustion of the conditioning program was two or three "invitational" track meets, and then the conference championship near the last day of school in May.

I was preparing for a spot in the mile relay. The

mile relay was one of the premier events of a high school track meet (we thought) along with the l00-yard dash and the mile run. The other relays, the speed, jumping and weight events counted for as many points, but the mile relay often turned out to be the showcase event.

The mile relay was performed by four runners, each running an equal distance — a quarter-mile, 440 yards. The second fastest quarter miler was usually started first, to try to give the relay team a bit of a lead. The third fastest runner ran second, hopefully to hold or extend that lead. The slowest runner was third. His job was to hold the team's position, or loose as little ground as possible.

The fourth man was the anchor man. His job was to win the race, whether he started ahead, in the middle or behind, he was supposed to run to win.

I ran third. I was the slow man. The problem with running the quarter mile is that it is a dash, but a high schooler's body hasn't yet developed enough to "dash" 440 yards. It runs out of gas at about 380 yards. The last 60 yards are absolute hell. The high school runners used to call it "hitting the wall," when the lungs are shrieking for air, the arms are turning numb, the legs are wobbly and the runner actually starts to black out. The track becomes a heaving blur, the finish line is a reeling, nauseous streak beyond which he sags to the ground, sliding along the cinders in his own vomit. That's what can happen to a high school kid if he runs the 440 all out.

On this day in May of l942, there were four teams entered in the conference championship mile relay. We knew that two of the teams were slower than we were. We had raced them before and beaten them handily. But the team from Milbank was tough. We had lost to Milbank in an earlier meet and lost to the same team at the conference championships a year earlier. Our team jogged around nervously in the infield, stomachs churning and fluttering, trying to keep our muscles warm, trying not to think about the excruciating, maximum effort we had committed ourselves to deliver.

Coach Doney came over from watching the weights competition to talk briefly to the team.

"You boys know how to run this race. You can win it. Just make sure those baton passes are perfect. Do it exactly the way we practiced. Concentrate hard on the baton passes. Do them right. Then run the best you can. It's a guts run, boys. It is entirely up to you. If you give it enough, you will win it. We are counting on you. You can do it."

He looked at each of us without smiling. "Good luck," he said.

Freddie Sanders was the first runner. Gordy Haug ran second. I was third, and Mike Insley, "Iron Mike," was the anchor man. We looked at each other with drawn faces.

The starter called for the teams to come to the line.

"Well, lets go bust our guts," Freddie said.

Freddie did his job. He came around about five yards ahead of the Milbank runner. Gordy Haug held the position. I could hear him choking and gasping as he came pounding up the stretch. I turned up the track and started to run. I felt the baton slap into my palm, and I sprinted toward the first turn. The Milbank third man was about a yard behind me on my right. I felt strange, as if the race was in slow motion, as if my feet wouldn't come down fast enough to start another stride.

As we pounded up the back stretch, reality began to return. I was gasping for air. My lungs were starting the familiar burning and hurting. My head felt light as

I came around the turn, now a yard behind the other runner. The pain in my lungs, my legs and my arms was becoming unbearable.

"I can't make it! I can't keep it up! It's too tough. I can't make it!" my mind was screaming. But my legs kept pounding, unguided by my reluctant brain. As I turned into the stretch to the finish line, I got "hit" properly. I felt I was blacking out. I couldn't feel my arms or legs, but my mind was now hysterically screaming, "Drive, drive, drive!" My vision began to blur.

I saw Mike jogging forward, his hand reaching back for the baton. Against the resistance of my fading body, I lunged forward and tucked the baton into Mike's outstretched hand. Mike the sprinter, the iron man, took off.

"I held him," my mind told me. "I held him. I didn't lose ground. I gave Mike a chance."

And a chance was all Mike needed. He gained steadily on the Milbank anchor runner and steamed in five yards in front.

Afterward, as our breathing returned to near normal, we stood in a circle near the center of the infield and grinned at each other.

"It was worth it," I said.

"It was one helluva thrill, guys. We'll probably never, ever have a time like this together again. It was just fantastic!" Freddie gasped.

And we never did. Mike was killed in a training accident in World War II. Freddie survived the war, but died in 1945 in Montana of some rare kidney disease. Gordy stayed home from the war because of a leaky heart valve, married and raised a wonderful family. I served a couple of years in the Air Force, went to college, then lived in several cities, following a career in advertising and publishing.

What remains of our high school class gets together every five years, recently to celebrate the fifty-fifth anniversary of our graduation. We never read the honor roll of the dead, but we think about them and those wonderful years together.

It's OK

Word came to Groton in 1944 that Johnny Bear had been killed on an ugly, blood-soaked beach in the Pacific. Freddie was in the navy then, Gordy was working in Aberdeen, and I was in the Air Force.

Freddie and I returned home in 1945, and Freddie went on to join his family in Montana, where he died suddenly of a kidney disease.

I was in Groton for a few months, getting ready to go to college. My parents had given up the farm and returned to teaching.

One day in late May, I decided I had some unfinished business to handle. The John Bear farm looked about like it had three years earlier. There was a small grove of tall, rustling cottonwoods, plus some gnarled box elder trees. There was an old Chevy parked in the driveway. The tires were up, the doors seemed to close, but the old car didn't show much in additional signs of life.

It was evening, and John Bear Day was sitting on a low porch on the south side of the house, facing the road. His chair was tilted back, and he watched me park my Dad's car and come slowly up the driveway. I thought he looked healthy, but old.

He rose, walked to the edge of the porch and held out his hand. I clasped it hesitantly, and shook.

"Hello, Mr. Bear."

"Howdy. You OK?"

"I'm fine, sir. You look good. How'd the winter treat you?"

"We got by OK. Got us a good wood burner in there, an' we had plenty 'a wood.

"I stopped by to set something straight," I said. I paused and kicked at the dirt of the driveway. John Bear watched me, and waited.

"Johnny wasn't driving the Model T the night Janey Ryan was hurt. I was in a tight spot, Mr. Bear. Someone else was driving, who was also a best friend. If I had cleared Johnny, I would have had to hang it on my other friend. So I chickened out. I didn't say anything.

"I'm going to tell people about it now, though. I got to set it straight. It was bad what they did to Johnny and you and your family. Bad what they said about him."

John Bear, with a dark, gnarled hand, tapped me on the shoulder. "Don't say nothing about it, Howard. Don't stir up no more trouble. I knowed Johnny didn't do it. Johnny was a good kid. He would have owned up to it. I knowed it, and his Ma knowed it. What them other people said don't make no difference. Just leave it be. Don't cause no more hurt."

"But I can't do that, Mr. Bear. Johnny doesn't deserve it. He was my friend. He was a great guy. The best there was."

"Yeah, he was a good kid. He's a good Indian now, he's dead." He paused a long time. "I wish I was dead, but I got to stay here an' look after my woman." John Bear looked away to the horizon, and there was a long silence. I watched his deeply lined face, dark and drawn.

"I don't know what to say, or what to do, Mr. Bear. I'm so sorry about everything."

"You're OK, Howard. You're OK. Don't feel bad, and don't do nothing about it. Just look after yourself."

I stood in the driveway, looking up at the somber man on the low porch. He slowly forced a smile and raised his hand, palm out, in the old salute. "It's OK, Howard. It's OK," he said.

I bowed my head and kicked again at the dust around my feet. Then I slowly raised my hand, palm out, and looked the proud old man in the face.

"So long, Mr. Bear."

"So long, Howard."

I went slowly back down the driveway, past the old Chevy, toward our car at the edge of the road. I looked back and he had returned to his chair, and was leaning forward with his forearms on his knees, staring at the splintered floor. Then he looked far out at the horizon, then back at me. He raised his hand once again in a final salute.

I never saw him again.

Under the Pine Trees

There is no air more pure anywhere else in the world, no sky more clear, no stars brighter than in the central plains of South Dakota. I've seen the night sky from many places on the planet — from a camp near a Maasai village on the edge of the Serengeti Plain in Africa, from a fishing camp near the Arctic Circle, from a boat tied to a lobster buoy ninety miles east of Montauk in the Atlantic. None compare to the night sky of the Dakotas. On a clear night, the Dakota skies produce a star show unsurpassed anywhere in the world.

Don't mind the dust that sometimes tints the air, swooped up by the occasional northwest winds sweeping across the open fields and ranges. That kind of dust isn't noxious. It isn't chemical. It has few germs or disease spores in it. It has no soot or smog in it. It is only soil — clean, healthy, fertile soil. It tastes gritty, but good. It smells wholesome when lodged in the nostrils. It washes off clean, with a scouring effect that leaves the skin cleaner than before.

The Groton cemetery lies out under those clear skies and bright stars, washed by the violent summer thunderstorms, swept clean by the steady prairie breeze, sterilized to absolute purity by the winter frost and snow.

It is a well-kept, orderly place, not very big.

Until about twenty years ago, there were two "sides" to this cemetery — Protestant in the north half; Catholic in the south half. Recently, partly because the Protestant section was getting full and partly because of a growing ecumenical harmony, Protestant graves are beginning to show up in the south half. Also, maybe it was because some of the old, hard-line priests and ministers have died off. (In the l940's they were still crossing the street to avoid having to speak to each other).

There are three narrow gates leading into the cemetery from the highway — one in the middle of the Protestant north, one in the same position for the Catholic south half, and one dead center leading to the flagpole in the middle of a circular, turn-around drive. The two drive-throughs on the wings lead to narrow trails that wind around between the rows of graves and return through the center gate. The outside gates are one car wide (one horse and buggy wide when they were built). The center gate is wider, but not wide enough to accommodate two cars, if there were ever such an occasion.

It is a slightly cramped, compact area, planned by the pioneers to accommodate a smaller community than had developed. It is well cared for.

Many of the trees on the north end are giant cottonwoods, the prairie "tree weed" that can survive almost anything but fire. Those magnificent trees, sometimes six feet or more around the trunk near the base, prevailed in this land because they were the survivors of the great droughts that periodically swept the Dakotas. The prairie ash was also an extremely durable survivor tree, but in its struggle to stay alive during the dry periods and the long, cold, winters, the ash became gnarled and stunted, seldom over twenty feet tall. The ash trees aren't majestic enough to guard graves, so there aren't many in the cemetery. They are ideal for farm shelter groves because they need virtually no care and form a dense wind break.

The attribute that makes this cemetery special are the pine trees. The people must have started planting pines in the early 1900's, because by the '30's and '40's, they were towering, full-bodied sentinels.

Pine trees are not indigenous to the open, flat prairie. The closest place that these trees grow naturally is in the lake country of Minnesota, two hundred miles northeast, and in the Black Hills, three hundred miles west. The pine trees survived and prospered in this cemetery by virtue of special care, a technique that was passed from one caretaker to the next. Water was their primary need when they were small, more water than the prairie climate could provide. As they grew taller, their long tap roots would go deep to find moisture. Also, they needed a light, preferably sandy soil, not prairie clay and gumbo. Fortunately, this cemetery was situated on a narrow strip of sandy soil that traced its winding way down from the north, and near the town turned east toward the low hills. Apparently it was the leading edge of a small glacier that had died there.

There was a shallow well in the cemetery against the back fence near the middle. It was adjacent to the shed that held the mower and the caretaker's hand tools. In a land of deep artesian wells, this shallow, hand-dug surface well was unique. The main reason for not going deep was to avoid the highly mineralized water that often came from the artesian wells. Although the water from that shallow well was generally considered unsafe for drinking, it was wonderfully refreshing on a hot, dusty Sunday afternoon to go to the well in the shade of the tall cottonwoods and pines and pump up the cool water. It was a hand pump, which in itself was a new experience for us children.

The water would gurgle deep in the well, then begin to pour from the spout on the pump as we heaved the pump handle up and down. Some of the water would miss the pail and fall to the dusty ground, forming little balls of water encapsulated in dust. The soil was so hot and dry, the water and soil wouldn't immediately mix. Instead the dust and water formed black "pearls," which would roll down the path.

Two of us would carry the heavy bucket of water down the dirt path to the gravel drive, then to the gravesites, and carefully pour it on the parched peonies and iris, and any annual flowers that might have been brought out and planted on Memorial Day. The flowers usually go quite dormant during the hot, dry months of July and August. The Sunday waterings, along with the trip to church, were an irregular ritual for our busy family, fighting for survival on the farm.

The caretaker watered the pine trees faithfully, though. In the earlier years, it was all done by hand, carrying two pails of water from the well to each tree, trudging back and forth, bathed in sweat. The workers didn't grumble and complain much about the watering. In that land, making something grow green and tall was an accomplishment, met with praise and appreciation.

During the drought and depression, families would go to the cemetery on hot, dry Sunday afternoons to enjoy the shade, the cool scent of pine trees, and the perfume of the flowers. It was a soothing, soul-cleansing communion between the living and the dead. The dead aren't pitied so much in that cemetery. They have a fine place, cool and fresh in the summer, neat and clean in winter, right by the highway, thus much less lonely than many of the farms and ranches out past the shimmering horizon.

My maternal grandfather, August Krueger, the immigrant from West Prussia, lies there beside Augusta, his wife, the bride from Wisconsin. They came to this land more than a hundred years ago. Sharing their space is Mick, the German boy who came here as a 14-year-old. He never married, and lived out his life on a lonely one-man farm.

Their daughter, my Mother, Lydia Jones is there, together with my Dad, the brave man with the withered arm. Also my sister Mary, beautiful Mary, who died during lung surgery while I was in high school. Many other relatives are there, and a few friends.

The seasons change. The winter winds drift cold, dry snow over them. In summer, the alternating wet and dry periods somehow nurture the coarse prairie grass that forms a benevolent blanket over the graves of the people resting there forever under the pine trees.

Howard Jones grew up on a farm in Eastern Dakota during the worst of the dust storms and the Great Depression. He attended a remote country school with never more than nine fellow students. After high school, the Air Force, college and a career in advertising and publishing, he moved to Florida to relax in the sun and write stories.